To

KAREN

HEART AND
SOUL

C.L. STEWART

HEART AND SOUL

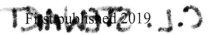

First published 2019

www.clstewart.co.uk

ISBN: 978-1-9993193-4-2

For D, L, C & A

You are all my light, my love, my life and I love you
with all my heart and soul.

ACKNOWLEDGEMENTS

Thank you to my family for your support and patience. You all mean the world to me and I hope I've made you proud.

I'd also like to thank my wonderful friend Liz. I know I've said it before, but you are the reason these books even made it at all. I'll never be able to thank you enough for all that you've done for me and I don't mean only with my books. You are a such special friend and I'm privileged to know you.

And lastly, I thank everyone who ever took a chance on an Indie Author and read their books. Without you dear readers our work would be swallowed up in the vastness of the bestsellers. I have been so lucky to connect with lots of readers on various social media platforms and in my daily life and the enthusiasm from everyone has been a huge motivator in times of self-doubt or writing fatigue. So, on behalf of all the indies in the world, I say to you all, you are wonderful, and your support is immeasurable

CHAPTER 1

HOSPITAL WAITING ROOMS ARE really, pretty depressing places. This one is no different. It doesn't matter that the walls are filled with posters of cute little babies and smiling mothers. The whole place is making me feel sick. As I stand next to the water cooler, holding the flimsy plastic cup in my hand, a very heavily pregnant woman and her partner walk in. I watch them as they sit down. She rubs her belly while he rubs her back. He tells her he loves her and that he is so proud of her. They look happy together.

Tears fall silently from my eyes and I turn away towards the window. It's dark outside and I can see my reflection in the glass. I look like shit. Turning to the side I look at my body's profile. I don't look any different and I don't feel any different. You would think I would know if I was pregnant without having to do a test. Charlie told me all about how she realised she was pregnant. The sore boobs, throwing up, missed periods and such. I have experienced none of these.

As it happens, I still don't even know. I didn't get a chance to look at the test and neither did Charlie. Right now, I am in the waiting room of the Royal Infirmary's Maternity unit while my friend is getting checked over by a midwife. This hospital is becoming far too familiar to me these days. Baby Georgie's timing is impeccable and she's not even here yet. Charlie is in labour and, according to the midwife, probably has been since yesterday.

I finish my cup of water and head outside to call Mark again. I've been unable to get hold of him since before we left Steven's apartment. Bugger it! Steven! I haven't called him. As soon as my phone comes to life it rings in my hand. It's Mark.

"Mark. Thank God."

"Shit Gina I've been trying to call for the last fifteen minutes, since I got your message. I'm freaking out here. What's happened? Is Charlie okay?"

"Mark..."

"I'm trying to get a flight organised but it's such short notice..."

"Mark..."

"...I've explained to my colleagues that I need to..."

Good God it's like talking to my mother, I can't get

a word in.

"MARK!" I shout and he stops talking.

"Shit, I'm sorry Gina, I'm panicking."

"I know. First of all, calm down. Charlie is at Glasgow Royal Infirmary and she is being checked over right now. I don't know how advanced things are, but she is in labour. I think she had just got off the phone to you and her waters broke in Steven's bathroom. I'm just about to phone Steven so I'll see if there is something he can do for you, okay? I'll call you back."

I can hear a sigh of relief on the other end of the phone.

"Thanks Gina, I'll keep the line open."

"Right, stay where you are and I'll call you back." We hang up and I call Steven. He answers on the second ring.

"Hey gorgeous. I was just thinking about you."

"Hey listen, Charlie's waters broke this afternoon, she's in labour. We're at the hospital now."

"Jesus Gina you should have called me earlier."

"I've only just managed to get a hold of Mark. He's still in London, he's having trouble getting a flight though."

"Leave that with me. I'll deal with it, I have his number. You go and be with Charlie. Is there anything she needs?"

"I think she really could do with having her hospital bag here but it's at her flat."

"I'll get Gerry to pick it up and I'll be there shortly okay."

"Thanks Steven, I really appreciate this."

"Anything for you babe you know that. I need to go and sort Mark out. Get back to Charlie. Love you Gina."

"Love you too Steven," I say as we hang up and the breath I take comes out stuttered.

I give myself a shake, I can't dwell on my own problems right now, my friend needs me.

Charlie is sitting up in bed reading a magazine when I get back to the ward.

"How did your examination go honey?"

"Well...I'm five centimetres and the contractions are coming along nicely apparently. I'm now in active labour. Gina you should try some of this stuff. It's amazeballs. Ha." Charlie's expression looks strange and she holds up a hose with a mouthpiece attached to it.

"What is it?"

"Gas and air. Best thing ever, I want to take it home," she laughs then abruptly throws her head back, her contraction quickly turning the laugh to a pained growl.

"Gina this is going to kill me."

"What about all the drugs you were going to have?"

"Fuck no, I've heard all these horror stories so I'm going without. Did you get a hold of Mark?"

"Yeah honey but he's having trouble getting out of London. Steven is going to help. Don't know what he will be able to do but he said he'd handle it. He is also getting Gerry to drop off your bag from your house."

Her smile is thankful.

"Gina I really need him here."

I can see she is getting distressed.

"I'm here for as long as you need me honey, okay?"

"Thanks Gina."

My phone pings with a text and I quickly pull it out of my pocket and turn it to silent before I get told off. "Oops. It's from Steven." I read it and smile at Charlie. "He says he got Mark a flight on a wee private plane doing an empty return journey to Glasgow. I have no idea what that means but he says the flight should get into Glasgow in about an hour."

"Thank God. Hear that Georgie?" Charlie says patting her belly. "Your daddy won't be long so you just stay in there as long as you can okay baby girl?"

"Can I get you anything honey? Do you want a drink?"

"No, I'm fine babe, I've got some here. Why don't we talk about the elephant in the room right now? And I don't mean me."

I don't think I can talk about this right now. I am having a hard enough time as it is surrounded by all these pregnant women and babies.

"Let's not."

"You're going to have to talk about it Gina. I can see it's eating you up."

Of course she is right. On one hand I know I have always wanted children but on the other it is way too soon. Steven and I have been through so much in the last few months we haven't had enough time alone to really get to know each other. I also don't know what his reaction will be. I don't even know if he wants kids.

"Oh Charlie, what am I going to do if that test is positive? What did you do with it anyway?"

"It's still sitting on the worktop in Steven's kitchen. If it's positive you'll just have to get on with it and Steven will too. Listen, you do know you are going to have to talk to him about this regardless of how it turns out don't you? God Gina these are getting painful."

Charlie grabs my hand and squeezes it tight. Her face contorts as she goes through her breathing exercises. When she is done she carries on talking as if nothing happened and we sit chatting and breathing through the contractions for the next hour and a half.

Eventually, the midwife joins us and as I stand to leave her room the door flies open. Mark has finally arrived and he rushes towards Charlie with tears in his eyes.

"Oh my God Charlie I am so sorry. I got here as fast as I could," he says to her, kissing her hand and turns towards me.

"Gina I can't thank you enough. You and Steven are the best. He got me a flight on a private plane, and he picked me up from the airport himself."

"Is he here?"

"Yeah, he's parking the car. I was out before he had even stopped."

Mark turns back to Charlie who is having another contraction. The midwife makes her comfortable and I give Mark's shoulder a squeeze.

"Right you two I'm going to find Steven. Good luck honey," I say to Charlie and kiss her head.

"Thanks Gina." She smiles at me and I blow her a kiss as I leave.

As soon as I'm out the door, the rush of emotion coursing through me takes my legs out from under me and I collapse in a heap by the door. The next voice I hear pulls me out of the darkness and I look up to see Steven's worried eyes.

CHAPTER 2

"GINA." STEVEN HELPS ME up and takes my hand. "Come with me." He leads me away from Charlie's room and down the hallway to the waiting room, thankfully it is empty. As he closes the door, he leans on it for a few seconds before turning around.

"It's been a bit of a day for you hasn't it?"

I nod and look into his eyes. Something is wrong. He is silent and although it is only for a few seconds it feels like hours. When he eventually speaks, he doesn't even look at me.

"Do you have something you need to tell me Gina?"

Fuck!

He puts his hand in his pocket and pulls out the pregnancy test. I think I am about to faint.

"Steven I am so sorry."

The way he is holding it means I can't see the result, but he can.

"Why are you sorry? Is this yours?"

I can't tell if he is angry or not and it is un-nerving me a little.

"Yes, it is, but I don't know what the result is." I bow my head.

This is the worst thing that could have happened to me today and I fear that either way this result is going to change things between us.

"Do you want to know what the result is?"

"Not really."

"Why?"

Because I don't want you to leave me. Because I don't want you to hate me. Because I love you. I know what I want to say but the words won't come out. I shrug my shoulders instead. I feel like a child who has been caught lying.

"Gina, look at me."

I do, slowly, and see a pained expression on his face.

"God Steven. What does it say?"

"Before I show you, I want you to know something. I love you Gina and no matter what, I will always be here. I told you I was never letting you go and I meant it."

I put my head in my hands.

"I'm so sorry, this is not how things were supposed to be."

"Gina, look."

I lift my head and look at the test. There, in the little window is one very clear pink line. Nothing else. It's negative. My insides should be having a party right now but all I feel is disappointment. It is the strangest feeling.

"You're not pregnant Gina."

"Yeah…I can see that," my tone is clipped.

"You're not pleased then?"

"I don't know Steven. I had mixed emotions about all this. My thoughts mainly centred around you though. I was worried about what you would say or do if it was positive. Like maybe you would be mad at me or that you wouldn't want a baby and would leave me. I would have understood you know, given what happened to you as a child."

He puts the test back in his pocket, holds my hands and looks into my eyes. "Gina, I told you before, you saved me from myself. I was quite happy to go on with my life on my own. Before I met you I would never even have considered having children. As you've said, I know what a horrible place the world can be and I would never wish that on any child. Meeting you changed that. You made me realise I actually have something to give and that there is some good in the

16

world."

"Are you disappointed Steven?"

He smiles and shrugs his shoulders. "I don't know really. When I found this in the kitchen I was shocked, but the more I thought about it the more I thought it wouldn't be the end of the world. I mean, yes, we probably would have had to move house and maybe have had a million more therapy sessions but we could make it work. It's a strange feeling but it has made me realise we have a lot to make up for. I want us to get back all those weeks we've lost and really get to know each other. It's been one drama after another and I'm ready for it all to be done."

And on cue I start crying. "Steven, you will make a wonderful father someday, I have no doubt. I'll make an appointment with the doctor and get different contraception, one I can't forget about." I swipe the tears from my cheeks and give him a small, teary smile.

"Come on let's get out of here. I told Mark to call as soon as there was any news."

***

The drive back to the apartment only takes around ten minutes and as soon as we are through the front door, Steven lifts me up so that I have to wrap my legs round his waist. He has me pinned against the door and we kiss each other so wildly our teeth clash. He lowers us to the floor and lays me down on the cold tiles. He quickly pulls off one of my boots and yanks my jeans and panties low enough to pull one leg off. I have no idea what has caused this to be so fevered and quite frankly I don't care.

Steven manages to get his jeans and boxers low enough to free himself and from somewhere, produces a condom. I was ready for him the moment he kissed me and within seconds he is inside me. I am close to orgasm quicker than I ever have been and it takes a mere four or five thrusts for him to get me there. Another few hard and fast plunges and he's done for too. As his body stills, I feel the need to come again and my hips move as if possessed. With each little movement, my body tightens. As I give in to its demands, I am filled with a sense of relief because I now know that no matter what this life might throw at us, this man loves me, and the feeling is absolutely mutual.

CHAPTER 3

THE TV IS ON and although I'm looking at it, I'm not taking anything in. My mind has been on a multitude of other things all day and I fear at some point it is going to overload. I am lying on the couch in the TV room with my head in Steven's lap. After our quick encounter in the hallway, we showered together and now I am waiting with bated breath to hear from Mark about Charlie's progress. I got a text about half an hour ago to say she had been taken to the delivery suite and that it wouldn't be long until baby arrives.

"Are you okay Gina?" Steven asks, stroking my hair.

I don't know, am I okay? I somehow feel empty inside. I had been so freaked out earlier in the day and I had actually convinced myself that the test was going to be positive. Seeing the negative result left me with mixed feelings. I really am going to need my therapy session on Tuesday, I have so many unresolved emotions over this and I really don't think Steven would understand.

"I'm fine, I'm just exhausted. It really has been a long day."

"Do you want to go to bed? I am pretty beat myself. Your dad whipped my arse today on that golf course. He really is good."

I smile. It's wonderful that he already has such a good relationship with my dad. "No, I want to hear about Charlie first. I won't be able to sleep unless I know everything is alright."

"Okay. Do you want something to eat? I'm going fridge raiding."

I give a little laugh and sit up.

"What's funny?"

"Do you know what I really would love right now? A McDonald's."

Steven laughs. "God Gina I can't remember the last time I went to McDonald's. Probably when I was a student. Go and get dressed, we'll go for a drive through."

I give him a huge smile, this is what I like. Normality. Its little things like this that makes a relationship. Hopefully from now on normality in our lives will be the norm and not the exception.

***

We both emerge from getting dressed and as soon as we see each other we end up in hysterics. I am wearing a pair of light, ripped, slouchy boyfriend jeans and a white T-shirt and Steven is a mirror image.

"Great minds think alike eh?"

"Or small minds seldom differ," I laugh and try to run away but he manages to slap my bum.

"Oww!" I squeal and run down the stairs.

He catches me at the bottom, grabbing me around the waist and pulls me in to his body. We stand looking at each other, both a little out of breath from taking the stairs so fast. He kisses my head.

"Beautiful girl," he whispers.

My smile is huge, and his words make my insides melt. *Please let this be the start of forever,* I silently pray to myself as Steven lets me go and takes my hand, leading us out the door.

***

McDonald's is only a short drive away. I actually can't believe we are taking an Aston Martin to a McDonald's drive thru. As we sit in the queue behind a Mini, a little giggle escapes my lips.

"What?" Says Steven, although I think he already knows what I am laughing at.

"We look like a couple of hobos who won the

21

lottery and can't stop doing the simple things they used to."

He turns to me and smiles. "Babe winning the lottery would never compare to winning you."

I laugh and make the universal *'don't make me sick'* signal. He smiles back at me. As we approach the speaker to place our order Steven shakes his head and shrugs.

"I don't even know what they sell here anymore. What are you having?"

"I want a large quarter pounder meal with extra fries and an apple pie."

"Jesus woman that's a lot of food."

"And mozzarella sticks if they have them." I give him a huge grin.

"Anything for you angel."

He winks at me and pulls up next to the speaker. The tinny voice rattles from the silver box.

"Welcome to McDonald's. Can I take your order please?"

"Yeah, we'll have two large quarter pounder meals, two extra fries, two apple pies and two mozzarella sticks please."

He's so out of his depth here that he can't even think for himself. It's rather cute if I'm honest. The voice repeats the order and asks what drinks we would like.

"Do you sell whisky?" Steven asks and laughs.

"Naw," comes the voice, short, clipped and not in the least bit amused.

Steven shrugs his shoulders. "Two Diet Cokes then please. I'll add the whisky later."

I laugh at him.

"That'll be £17.92 at the first window thanks."

Steven turns back to me. "Wow, that's cheap."

The speaker clicks off and we drive to the window. It is closed and the young guy at the till behind it looks like he has lost the will to live. He looks about nineteen or twenty.

"Jesus check this guy out. Nothing like being happy at your job," Steven says.

I cock my head at him. "I wonder what his story is. Do you think he's a student? Charlie and I had some extremely questionable jobs when we first started at Uni."

He is about to answer when the young guy opens the window. He stutters as he asks for the money all the while eyeing the car.

"Nice wheels mate," he says to Steven with a genuine smile on his face as he takes the cash from him.

I think this has made his night. His smile disappears when a manager comes up beside him and starts shouting at him in front of us.

"Seriously James, this is the third order that's been

sent back tonight. Let this be a warning, one more and you'll be disciplined."

The bleached blonde, wearing far too much make-up, walks away muttering to herself leaving poor James standing there with a red face. He looks like he is about to cry. I feel terrible for him.

"Here's your change sir. Collect your order at the next window," says James and closes the window.

We drive to the next window and collect our food. Steven is very quiet as he takes the drinks and the bag and hands them to me. He thanks the girl at the window, who is giving him puppy eyes, and drives off. After a few minutes of silence, I can bear it no longer.

"Steven, what's up?"

He shakes his head as he brings the car to a stop outside the apartment building.

"I feel bad for that young guy at McDonalds. The way that perma-tanned bitch talked to him was awful. No wonder he looked miserable."

"Yeah she was a bit of a cow wasn't she? Now what's really eating you?"

"You're too observant Ms Harper. I'm just feeling strange doing this...normal stuff."

I give a little laugh. "What McDonald's? It's only food, I wouldn't take it too seriously but if we don't get in and eat it soon it's going to be freezing."

He smiles at me and gets out of the car and opens

my door. "This way gorgeous."

As soon as we are in the kitchen, I empty the bag and round up the stray fries from the bottom, shovelling them into my mouth. Steven laughs at me as he sits at the table. My phone vibrates in my pocket and almost makes me choke on the salty fries. It's Mark and I don't even swallow my food before I answer.

"Mark. Tell me tell me tell me."

"What's with your voice?"

"McDonald's, now how is my bestie?"

He laughs at me. "We are the proud parents of a little baby girl born at five past eleven this evening, weighing seven pounds one ounce. Gina she is just perfect."

My eyes well up. I am so happy for them. "How is Charlie?"

"She's doing fine. Baby is feeding from her already. I swear she came out making sucking noises. I'm so proud of her Gina, she did it all without pain relief. I nearly fucking fainted."

"I'm so happy for you. Steven and I will come and visit tomorrow afternoon okay." I look at Steven and he smiles with a nod.

"Thanks Gina, I'll let Charlie know. And listen, thanks so much for everything you and Steven did today, I'm so glad I made it here. I promise I owe you guys."

"Don't be silly now go and be with your family, we'll see you tomorrow." We hang up and I stand on the spot clutching the phone to my chest.

"Hey, are you okay?" Steven says pulling my hand towards him.

"Yeah it's been a very draining day. I'm glad it's Sunday tomorrow, can we sleep in?"

"Sounds good to me." He takes a bite of his burger and closes his eyes. "God Gina, I forgot how good fast food tastes."

"Yeah it is good but please stop making sex noises to your burger, I might get the wrong idea."

He fires a French fry at me, and I stick out my tongue.

CHAPTER 4

LOOKING DOWN AT THE porcelain doll-like face of baby Georgie, I am overwhelmed with love for her and her mother. Charlie is sitting up in bed smiling at me.

"Charlie she is perfect," I whisper.

"Isn't she? I can't stop looking at her Gina. I still can't believe she's here."

"How was the labour?"

"Well I was fine. Apparently, it was a pretty straightforward delivery. It was damn painful; actually, it was like a burning sensation more than anything. I kind of forgot the pain as soon as I set eyes on her. Mark was a bloody wreck. I was considering throwing him out at one point. I thought he was going to faint."

"Aww poor Mark. It is quite traumatic seeing

someone give birth you know. I imagine it's even worse if it's someone you love."

Charlie shakes her head. "I'm sorry honey, I completely forgot all about that."

"No don't be. I'd much rather forget and get to know this little princess. Can I hold her?"

"Of course you can Auntie Gina," Charlie smiles at me.

I tentatively lift her little baby in my arms and in a matter of seconds I am overwhelmed with emotion. She is so tiny and perfectly formed. I take a seat beside Charlie's bed and we chat about all sorts until Mark comes in with Steven.

"Hey daddy, your daughter is so beautiful," I say to Mark who looks at me with a huge beaming smile on his face.

"Yes, she absolutely is." I hand her over to him. "I'm going for a coffee, anyone want anything?"

Steven is the only one who takes up my offer as he sits beside Mark. I am so happy. It's good to have something nice happen for once.

I buy two coffees from the nearest vending machine and head back with a smile on my face. When I walk back into Charlie's room the sight that greets me almost floors me and I don't know if it is from shock or love. Steven is holding baby Georgie on his knees with his hand behind her head and he is stroking her tiny cheek with his other hand. He is sitting there staring at her. Charlie and Mark are nowhere to be seen. My heart is about to burst right out of my chest. Steven turns and smiles at me and I take a seat next to him.

"That suits you," I nod at him.

It really does. He looks so at ease holding this tiny human.

"Hmm," is all he says and carries on gazing at Georgie.

"Where is everyone?"

Steven motions to the bathroom door. "Mark is helping Charlie shower, so I said I'd babysit for a wee while."

"That was nice of you." I place the coffees down on Charlie's bedside cabinet and pull my chair in closer to him.

We both sit looking at the baby and I wonder what he is thinking. I am thinking about how disappointed I was that my test was negative. Looking at Steven with Georgie I know I was right when I said he would be a good dad and that has a lot to do with the fact that he knows what a dad shouldn't be.

"How can anyone not love their child Gina? It's supposed to be the most primal instinct there is."

"You know, anyone can bear a child but not everyone has a good enough heart to love them. What did you feel when you first held Georgie?"

"Love. But I don't understand why. She's not mine or related to me so why did I feel that?"

"It's because you have a beautiful heart Steven. You love her because she is the daughter of a friend. Okay, I know Charlie is my best friend, but you have gotten to know her and come to love her as a friend too. Give yourself some credit Steven, you do love those close to you."

He leans in and kisses my cheek. "I love you gorgeous. Someday, you and I will make beautiful babies."

And there goes my heart, bursting with love for this beautiful soul. The bathroom door opening startles me, and I turn and see Charlie and Mark emerging. She looks invigorated after her shower. She gets back into bed and Steven hands Georgie back to her.

"We will get going honey and leave you to it. I need to get working on my submission for the art gallery. I need to email it all away today."

"Gina, I forgot all about that."

"Yeah, Ellen was good enough to give me an extension on the closing date considering the reason I missed it."

I shrug my shoulders as if it doesn't bother me but inside, I'm dying. Every time I think about what happened to me, I am filled with a sense of dread.

"That's brilliant. You need to let me know as soon as you hear anything. We'll be there for your opening day. Now get out of here my baby needs feeding and I'm not flashing my tits in front of your boyfriend."

I look at Steven whose face has gone a lovely puce colour.

"Charlie you maniac." I laugh at her and give her a kiss on the cheek and then kiss Georgie on the head. "See you soon little one."

We all say goodbye and Steven and I leave to head home. He takes my hand and links our fingers together as we walk down the corridor.

***

I have read the email on my computer screen about fifty times. My photos are ready to go. I have added some of Kelvingrove Park and the university buildings to my shots of the Aurora from Harris. I'm so nervous about submitting them now that every time I read over the email a little more doubt creeps into my mind. I have another four hours until my deadline passes so I think a little time away from my laptop will help.

Steven has decided to go to the gym for a few hours. I think the visit to the hospital today has knocked him out of sorts. He uses a gym close to where he lives, or close to where we live. God, I don't know when I'll get used to that. I know he probably owns it

31

or at least has a hand in it. It has occurred to me lately that he seems to only frequent places he has a vested interest in. The Winter Ball we attended in December was no exception. He was the mystery business that contributed to the night providing all the food, drinks and the waiting and bar staff. The trip to McDonald's took him right out of his comfort zone.

I pour myself a glass of wine and take it through to the TV room. Flicking on the TV I take a sip of my wine and immediately wish I hadn't. It's disgusting. It must be corked. I take it through to the kitchen and dump it in the sink. I decide on a hot chocolate instead.

I've managed to watch two full episodes of Grey's Anatomy and one of Modern Family and I'm now reluctantly standing in the kitchen in front of my laptop. It's now or never. I know I need to do this, but I am terrified. The sound of the front door opening makes me jump.

"Hi honey, I'm home."

I give a little laugh. Normality. It's nice. "I'm in the kitchen darling."

Steven appears at the door and I turn to greet him. OH! Well that's a sight for sore eyes. He has navy blue tracksuit bottoms on and a grey vest... covered in sweat. It really should be disgusting but I am finding it the hottest thing ever right now.

"H...hi. Ehm..."

Oh my God. I have seen this man naked. What the hell is wrong with me?

"Everything okay?" He smiles at me.

I give myself a mental shake. I need to deal with the email right now; I'll deal with Steven later.

"Yeah, I'm just trying to get up the courage to send this email to Ellen, I only have about fifteen minutes before the deadline is up."

"Do you want me to read over it for you?"

"Yes please. I keep doubting myself and if I read it again, I'm going to end up deleting it."

He dumps his bag on the floor and sits down at the table in front of the laptop. I stand where I am watching his reaction. When he touches the track pad, I think he is scrolling down the page until I hear the familiar whoosh of an email being sent.

"My God please tell me you didn't just do what I think you did?"

He smiles. "Gina, the email is perfect, the photos are brilliant, you are amazing. Please stop doubting yourself."

I sit down next to him. He is right, my photos are good, and I really do need to have more faith in myself.

"Okay thanks. Now I want to forget about it. You need a shower mister. Want me to wash your back?"

He smiles a wicked grin and pulls me off my seat right onto his knee so that I am straddling him. He pulls my head down, kissing me so deeply my lips swell. He stands up and lifts me with him, my legs wrapping round his waist.

"You can wash more than my back gorgeous."

I laugh as he carries me upstairs.

CHAPTER 5

MY LIGHTS ARE ALL in place and the white paper background is up. Charlie's living room looks like a professional studio. My camera is ready to go. All we are waiting for is Georgie. The little diva who decided, just as Charlie was going to lay her down on the beanbag, that she needed a nappy change. While I am waiting, I take a few pictures of some of Georgie's little toys and clothes. This photoshoot is a gift for Charlie and informal pictures like these will be ideal for the photobook I'm going to make. Georgie is just a week old and watching Charlie with her makes me burst with pride. She is such a good mum.

"Sorry Gina. She takes her timing from her daddy."

"It's okay. I've done loads of these new-born shoots. Babies are fine, its toddlers that are the problem. They get into everything. I did a shoot once with the brattiest kid on the planet and a mother who didn't have an ounce of sense. See the big light there?" I point at the big backlight.

Charlie nods.

"He pulled on the cable for it and ended up pulling the whole thing over, burst the bulb and wrecked the outer shade. His name was Marshall. Apparently when she had him, she was in love with Eminem. She thought calling him Eminem was a bit too over the top, so she named him Marshall instead because that's his real name."

Charlie shakes her head. "Some people are bloody idiots. Mark's mum hates Georgie's name. I think it's beautiful, but Ann says it's a boy's name."

I put on a mock pout. "How dare she! Georgie is a gorgeous name."

"She's doing my head in. I'm so grateful that I have her here because my mum is so far away, but she thinks because she's had kids, she knows everything. I've started just nodding and agreeing with her."

"Best thing to do to save arguments. Little madam is asleep so let's get going."

***

We spend the next hour wrapping and unwrapping Georgie, posing her, dressing her, placing her on props and all the other cute things that come with a new-born

36

photo shoot. These have always been my favourite. All you need to do is make sure the baby is asleep and just take everything very slowly. They are the most relaxing photo shoots to do. Doing this one makes me realise how much I love my job. I also get a few lovely shots of Charlie and Georgie together.

We have agreed that we will do another one when she is about six months old and then a first birthday one. I know I won't be able to leave it at that and I will probably do so many milestones that I will end up photographing her wedding when she is grown up and probably doing her own babies' photo's too.

"Thanks so much for today Gina, I've been cooped up in here since we got out of the hospital on Monday. Mum and Nikki will be here this coming Monday, but they are only staying five days. They need to get back and prepare for the move back to the UK."

"I can't wait to see them. You can bring Nikki to Glasgow and we can give her the grand tour and show her the flat."

"That's what I was planning. You know me well honey. Nikki has an interview on Wednesday over on the Clydeside, at the Broomielaw I think, so we will be in Glasgow then."

We sit chatting over coffee as Georgie sleeps in her little swinging chair beside us.

"How is everything going anyway? Is she feeding

okay now?"

"Yeah but no thanks to the bitch of a midwife who came to see me on Wednesday. I had only been home two days and I was quite emotional because she wouldn't feed on the Tuesday night. We ended up giving her a bottle of formula because I was worried she was going to starve. That horrible woman actually called me a silly girl. She said, *'you will mess up her feeding if you introduce a bottle and formula too early'.* Mark was going to throw her out of the house."

"What a cow."

"She was but I've not had her again and as of tomorrow we'll have a health visitor coming instead so I'm much happier about that. So, tell me how are things with you and Steven since you moved in?"

"Well since I have been practically living with him since before Christmas, it's really not that much different. Except for the fact that he has given me a whole side of his wardrobe."

My phone vibrates on the table. "Gerry is on his way back to pick me up. I'm so glad he had the Range Rover today, I would never have fitted all this equipment in the Bentley."

"Ooh listen to you, we'll be calling you the three car Parkers soon."

"Ha ha you can if we ever get married but it will need to be four. He has one in the Hebrides as well."

Charlie rolls her eyes. "Bitch."

I don't even know if that is all the cars he has, there could be more. We are still finding out so much about each other.

***

Gerry drives me home from Charlie's and helps me inside with all my equipment.

"Would you like a cup of tea or coffee Gerry?" I ask as we unload the last of the stuff from the car.

"Coffee would be lovely Gina thanks."

Sitting down at the kitchen table with two steaming mugs of coffee I give Gerry a little half smile.

"What's wrong love?" He asks.

"Gerry, I hate doing this, but I wanted to ask you about Steven."

"What do you want to know? Remember I love my job and want to keep it."

I shake my head and shrug my shoulders.

"Can I tell you something about him instead of you asking? Something I don't think very many people know." He asks.

I nod.

"I started working for Steven almost two years ago, but I've known him for a lot longer. He used to volunteer at a hospice centre for terminally ill children when he was at University. That's how I met him. My son developed leukaemia when he was three."

God that's awful. I didn't even know Gerry had a son. He fishes in his pocket and pulls out his wallet. Opening it he shows me a picture of a little blonde-haired boy with a massive grin on his face.

"This picture was taken on his third birthday. Three months later he was diagnosed and two years after that he passed away. That was seven years ago. I met Steven when he was twenty. Adam was five and by that time he was terminal. Steven used to come into the unit every day after Uni and was there all day on his days off. Adam loved him to bits."

My heart breaks and I understand the relationship between Steven and Gerry a bit better now.

"Gerry I am so sorry." I put my hand on his and try as hard as I can not to cry.

"Thanks honey. I do miss him dearly, but you know he was such a happy wee boy even when he was ill. Steven was at lectures the day Adam died and we had to give him the bad news when he got there. He was so cut up about it. He was the same when any of the kids passed away, but Adam really got to him. I think it was because he was one of the youngest kids there at the time. That was the last day Steven went to the centre."

"Oh God."

"I know Gina, he is a very private guy when it comes to showing his caring side."

"So how did you end up working for him then?"

"We kept in touch after Adam died. My wife and I had been growing apart whilst Adam was sick and when he died it completely broke us. I moved out and we got divorced quite soon after. When Steven graduated, he set up his own business and called me to say as soon as he had himself settled there was a job waiting for me. And you know that boy was true to his word."

This is a lot to take in. This is the guy who says he doesn't know if he has any love to give because he was never loved. God if he would only open his eyes he'd see.

"Thank you for telling me Gerry and I promise this is between you and me. If Steven wants to tell me himself so be it."

"He's a great guy Gina, he would help anyone out at the drop of a hat. He was really gutted when Cheryl threw everything back in his face after he tried to help her. There are just some people in this world who can't be helped." He takes a long sip of his coffee.

"I think Cheryl is too set in her ways," I say.

"He cares for you a great deal you know. I've never seen him as happy as when he talks about you. I'm so glad he has finally found someone to truly make him happy, he deserves it."

I nod my head and smile.

"I love him so much Gerry. He got me out of the darkest time of my life and I don't know how I'll ever thank him properly."

"Making him happy is enough. Right, I am going to need to go and park up the Range Rover. Steven needs me tonight and the Bentley needs a wash."

Funny he didn't say there was anything going on tonight. I thought this was going to be a quiet Saturday in for us. I say goodbye to Gerry and head upstairs for a shower. I have a lot to process after Gerry's revelations. I really have bagged myself a good man.

CHAPTER 6

DATE NIGHT. A TERM coined by couples with children or professional couples who never get five minutes alone with each other. Well I don't care; tonight I'm using it. Steven and I spend a lot of time together but it's mostly at home or with other people so tonight he is taking me on a date. Gerry knew all along when he was with me this afternoon. I knew I caught something in his eyes when he mentioned Steven needing him to drive tonight.

"So, what's on the menu at Black tonight then?"

I ask as we make our way across the West End. I love the nightclub Steven owns and tonight is the first time we have been there together, just the two of us.

"Whatever you want gorgeous. The chef will make you anything."

He lifts my hand to his lips and I feel the heat

emanating out across my knuckles. I am seeing him in a new light after my chat with Gerry today.

"Hmm that could be interesting."

"That's us here folks," says Gerry as he halts the car at the kerb and gets out to open the door.

As we get out of the car, I am about to thank Gerry when a flash goes off in my face. I look questioningly at Steven as I notice more photographers. *Bloody paps!* There must be someone famous in the club tonight. Steven smiles at me when he sees me looking at them.

"Yes, there's a party in the VIP lounge tonight." He tells me, as if reading my mind.

"Who is it do you know?"

"Some singer. I think she was on the X Factor or something. One of those ones who didn't win but got famous because Simon Cowell gave her a record deal anyway. Money makes money."

I'm intrigued. We might get to rub shoulders with celebrities tonight. We go in through the main door and straight to our booth. I say 'our booth' because anytime we have been here this is where we have sat. The place looks different tonight. The stage is dimly lit and there are six silver chairs on it with a black rope sitting on each.

"What's going on in here tonight?" I ask Steven as we take our seats.

"It's just a little after dinner entertainment." His

44

smile is very mischievous, and my interest is piqued.

"What type of entertainment?"

"You'll see."

He's enjoying messing with me. A waiter appears at our side.

"Good evening Mr Parker, Ms Harper what can I get you to drink?"

"Did the Macallan come in today Thomas?" Asks Steven.

"Yes sir, I believe Cerys was here and dealt with the delivery."

"Great can you bring the Lalique to the table with two glasses and a jug of water? Did she put the 1926 in the safe?"

"Yes sir she did."

"That's great. That will be all."

Thomas backs away from the table and leaves to get the drinks.

"So…we are having whisky then?"

"I've been waiting for these for a while now. Wait till you taste this one Gina it is stunning. It's a fifty-five year old. The other one is from 1926 and I had to buy that one at an auction, we won't be drinking that one."

Thomas returns to the table with a mahogany box, two glasses and a little crystal jug of water. Steven opens the box and lifts out the whisky from the satin lined interior. It is a beautiful crystal decanter bottle with an amber coloured stopper. It screams elegance and I dread to think how much it cost. I watch as Steven pours a measure into each glass and cuts them with a few drops of water. He slides one over to me and we both hold them up.

"Cheers my beautiful girl."

"Cheers handsome."

The whisky is exquisite and slides down my throat with ease leaving a fiery, nutty aftertaste.

"God…this is nice Steven."

"Yes, it is. I do like a good whisky."

Another waiter approaches the table to take our food order.

"Good evening Mr. Parker, Ms. Harper."

"Good evening Michael, Gina have you decided what you would like to eat tonight?"

I had been enjoying the whisky so much I forgot about the food. "Eh I don't know. I think being given a choice is a bad idea. Umm...steak. Rib eye if you have it. Medium rare."

"Very good ma'am. And for you sir?"

"I'll have the seafood linguine please."

"I'm enjoying this by the way." I say to Steven when we are alone.

"Me too it's nice to be normal."

I smile at him as he takes my hand in his, rubbing my knuckles back and forth with his thumb. He looks contemplative. His furrowed brow makes me wonder if something is wrong. I think back to something Nate said when we visited him together. *'Talk often, ask what the other is thinking. Even if you don't like the answer'*. I decide he is right.

"Is everything okay?" I ask quietly.

He smiles and nods. "Yeah, it's just... well I keep thinking normal is not right and that something is going to come along and ruin this."

I can't help myself. I let out a little laugh. "God Steven you sound like me. Funnily enough I spoke to Nate about this on Tuesday. After Charlie having the baby and the pregnancy scare and every other bloody thing that's happened to us over the last while I was having a hard time accepting that things could ever be normal for us."

Steven smiles, a slow knowing smile. "And what was the verdict then?"

"I kind of answered my own question. We've been through so much already that it doesn't matter what happens now. I don't think anything could break us. Nate says there is no such thing as normal anyway. Normality is what you make it, so that's what we do. We choose what is normal to us and just go with it."

"I suppose he's right. You know something Gina Harper?"

"What?"

47

"You are my normal, no matter what."

We are interrupted as our food is delivered to the table and we chat and eat for the next half an hour until I can't stuff anymore into my stomach. As our plates are cleared from our table I gesture to the stage.

"So, are you going to tell me what's going on in here tonight then?"

"After dinner entertainment, I already told you," says Steven as he checks his watch. "It's actually about to start. Come and sit over here beside me."

He pats the seat beside him, and I move obligingly, sitting as close as I can to him without climbing into his lap.

The place is absolutely packed tonight and the noise of chatter and clinking glasses echoes all around us. As the lights of the club dim, the noise stops abruptly. It's a strange atmosphere and I am starting to feel a little apprehensive about what this entertainment could be. The stage area is plunged into complete darkness. I look questioningly at Steven who simply smiles wickedly at me. Music starts to play. It's a sexy, sultry tune and as the lights come up on the stage, I understand what this act is and what the purpose of the chairs are. It looks like it could be a burlesque act, but I have never seen anything like this.

There are six women on the stage standing behind the chairs holding on to the backs with both hands.

They are all bent forward. Their outfits are simple. Black satin knickers and black satin bras. The black fishnet stockings add a dark sexiness to it. The thing that really strikes me about this is that they are all tied to the chair backs with black rope. The dancers all move to the music, swaying their backsides in unison. My breath catches in my throat when six men, wearing nothing but black jeans and carrying what looks like black satin scarves, appear on stage behind the women.

I am utterly mesmerised by this stage show. The women are blindfolded with the scarves and now starts an extremely erotic dance routine that captures the attention of everyone in the room. The way they move is fluid and elegant and obviously well-rehearsed. It is sexy but not tacky. The women all dance and move around the chairs, tied to them the whole time. I can't take my eyes off the ropes. I wonder what it's like to be blindfolded and tied up like that.

As the act comes to an end, I feel myself exhale long and low and Steven notices it too. He puts his hand on my knee and rubs his pinkie under the hem of my skirt. I realise how turned on I am because that slight touch from Steven is making me want to jump him in the middle of this packed club.

"Did you enjoy that?" Steven whispers so close to my ear that my hair moves under his breath.

"It was... different," I reply and turn my head to

look at him.

I can feel my face flush and I know he senses it. He edges his hand higher up my thigh until his pinkie is skimming the edge of my knickers. The club is still in semi darkness and the location and angle of this VIP booth means that no one can see what he is doing. He keeps doing this to me even as Thomas comes to the table to ask if we are okay for drinks. As Steven talks to him, ordering us iced water, he pushes his finger inside my knickers and skims my clit making me bite my lip. He moves his finger back and forth and I can feel my body trembling. He keeps talking to Thomas, knowing full well what he is doing to me. Knowing full well how much I want to let go. Before too long I can't hold out any more. Obviously sensing my impending orgasm, Steven presses his finger just that tiny bit harder and I am done for. I bite hard on my lip and close my eyes. It is all I can do not to scream the place down.

As I regain my composure, I open my eyes and see that Thomas has left our table. I look at Steven whose eyes are aflame with lust.

"Come with me," he says, his voice gruff and strained.

He stands up and pulls me from the booth, almost dragging me on my jellied legs towards the part of the club that houses his office. As soon as he has me through the door, he has me pinned up against it and my knickers are all but ripped off me, my skirt hitched up to my waist. Quicker than I can even think he has a condom on and is lifting me off my feet. As he slides inside me, I know I am able to enjoy this freely since we don't have an audience this time.

"Steven!" I shout, his name on my lips a cathartic release.

He rams himself hard into me and I feel the familiar tension spread all over my body. My hands are round his neck and I am holding on for dear life. I love how he makes me feel, like there is nothing else on this earth but us. He squeezes my bum hard and I let out a high-pitched squeal of delight. Every move he makes hits my clit dead on and the angle we are at means he is hitting the most deliciously sweet spot inside me. It's a double whammy for my senses and I can't control my wanton body. As I climax around him, I feel him pour his release into me and we both shudder together against the door.

"You're fucking killing me woman," Steven pants against my shoulder as we regain our equilibrium.

"Seriously? Mr Wayward Fingers...I'm killing you? I'm telling you right now if Thomas didn't know what was going on at that table, he must be a bloody virgin."

Steven laughs a low vibrating sound as he moves

back from me slightly. He discards the condom in the waste bin next to the desk, and bends down and has me step in to my knickers. He pulls my skirt back down to where it should be. Sorting his own clothes, he smiles at me.

"Let's get back to the table, there's plenty more entertainment to come."

"I liked what we've just seen actually." I can feel my face reddening.

"Is that so? What did you like about it?" He knows exactly where this is going.

"The ropes." I reply shyly, not able to look him in the eye.

"I've got rope. Lots of it," says Steven as he takes my hand and leads me out the door.

We sit back at our table, as a drag act is finishing up a rendition of 'I Love the Nightlife'. It's fabulous and there are people on the Dance floor. As the act finishes a compère appears.

"Ladies and gentlemen, it gives me great pleasure to introduce the next act tonight. We are very privileged to have this man play for us this evening. Let me tell you, he doesn't play for just anyone. Put your hands together for our very own host...Mr. Steven Parker!"

I turn to Steven wide eyed as a massive round of applause spreads throughout the club. He stands and holds out his hand to me. I shake my head, but he is not taking no for an answer. He grabs my hand and pulls me up from my seat, leading me to the stage. We take the steps up on to the dimly lit stage and Steven settles me on a bar stool which is placed next to the piano. I chance a glance at the audience and see some of them leaning in to whisper to each other. They are obviously talking about me. '*Who is she? Why is she up there? What is he doing with her?*'

Steven takes his seat behind the piano and runs his fingers over some keys. "Good evening ladies and gentlemen. Allow me to introduce my girlfriend Gina."

The whole place erupts in applause and chatter and I can feel my face burning. I hate being the centre of attention, especially in front of strangers.

"Thank you, thank you," Steven says into the microphone. "I am going to sing a couple of songs the first of which I am dedicating to you Gina. You are an amazing woman and you make me want to be the best I can be."

I smile at him, my love for this man overflowing from my heart. He starts to play the first few bars of the song and I recognise it immediately. It's a Billy Joel song. *'She's Got A Way'.*

"She's got a way about her, don't know what it is, but I know that I can't live without her."

We look directly at each other as he sings, and the

words of this song give me a lovely warm feeling all over. I am overawed by how good he is at playing and singing. His voice is amazing. As he sings the last few lines, I feel a tear fall from my cheek and land on my hand. He has made me feel like the most special person on the planet and my emotions are hard to hold on to. When he is finished, he winks at me.

"I love you Gina Harper, I always will."

I jump down off the stool and go to him. He pulls me down onto his lap and kisses me as applause and cheering engulfs the air.

"I love you too," I whisper and as I look at the audience, I see we have been given a standing ovation. God I am so embarrassed. I laugh and bury my face in his neck.

"I'm going back to the table for your next number babe. This attention is too much for me."

He smiles at me as I leave the stage and take my seat. As he starts to sing the next song, all I can do is look on in awe.

CHAPTER 7

"SHIT! STEVEN." I SCREAM at the top of my voice. I think I'm going to start hyperventilating. I re-read the email once more; just to be sure I am actually seeing what is written there.

From: Markham, Ellen [Ellen.Markham@mpgalleries.co.uk]
To: 'Georgina Harper'
Subject: Photography Showing at Kelvingrove Art Gallery

Hi Gina,
Thank you very much for your submission of your work to be exhibited at Kelvingrove. It gives me great pleasure to inform you that your photographs have been accepted to be part of the exhibition. The event will run from 28th Feb - 24th April. I would be grateful if you could get back to me ASAP to discuss the presentation of the pieces. Congratulations Gina.

Kind Regards
Ellen Markham
Markham Ponsonby Galleries

I can't quite take it in. They want my work. My work is going to be exhibited in Kelvingrove art gallery. I hear Steven running up the stairs and I lift my laptop and run to the door almost crashing into him.

"Jesus Gina what's up?"

"Oh. My. God. Read this," I say forcing the laptop into his hands.

"Woah calm down. Let me sit down."

We both go back into the office and he sits at his desk. As I watch him read, I flit restlessly from foot to foot next to him. When he is finished, he looks up with a huge smile on his face.

"Come here you wonderful woman." He pulls me down onto his lap and kisses me. "Well done, I am so proud of you."

"I can't believe this Steven, finally things are going well for me and we are doing good, aren't we?"

"Yeah I could get used to this normal," Steven laughs. "I need to go into the office this afternoon. I'm formally withdrawing from the Seattle project today, so I'll be there a while."

Steven had decided to give up on the Seattle building project after surveying the site. With everything that went on in the days following, he said he knew it was the best thing to do. Since my close call he has been rather protective of me, not wanting to leave me alone for too long and fussing over me. It's nice although I know it is partly out of guilt as well as love. I have tried to tell him that I don't blame him for what happened to me, but I understand that it's something he needs to deal with himself.

"I'll be fine. I'm going to get in touch with Ellen as soon as possible to see what I need to do now. I didn't think she would take me on to be honest."

"And why wouldn't she? You're very good at your job Gina, stop putting yourself down all the time. Have faith in yourself. It's not arrogant, not if you really *are* good at it. I can't wait to see the exhibition."

"Me too. I have to call Charlie and let her know. After all it was her who introduced me to Ellen in the first place."

Steven nods his agreement.

"She's a good friend to you Gina. I really like her a lot. And Mark. In fact, we have agreed to meet up and go to a rugby game next weekend."

"Is this the start of a bromance?" I laugh although I am glad they have both hit it off with each other.

Mark is a good guy and I know he really respects Steven especially after he helped get him back on time to see his little girl being born.

"Right I'm going to call Charlie and then Ellen. I think I might just take a wander along to the gallery this afternoon if the weather stays nice. I'll get some pictures in the park too."

"Cool you can walk me to work then, like a normal couple."

His smile is infectious, and I find myself revelling

in all this normality. It's nice to belong somewhere again and not feel disconnected from my whole life.

Charlie's phone goes to voicemail when I try to call. I assume she will probably be asleep or with her mum and Nikki, so I don't try again. I'll let her call me back when she's free. I try Ellen instead. She answers on the third ring.

"Hello Ellen Markham."

"Hi Ellen, it's Gina Harper here."

"Gina thanks for getting back to me honey. How are you?" Her voice is friendly and welcoming.

"I'm great Ellen, thanks so much for taking me on, I can't even begin to tell you how happy I am."

"Darling your photographs are some of the best we have seen in a very long time. Those ones of the Northern Lights are absolutely stunning. In fact, Simon and I have decided you will have the main exhibit space."

I am totally gobsmacked. I can't make my mouth form words.

"Gina, are you still there honey?" Ellen's concerned voice snaps me out of my daze.

"Yes, sorry Ellen. I'm just a little shocked. Thank you so much, this is more than I could ever have wished for."

"I know talent when I see it Gina and you have it in bucket loads. I am going to be doing a wall plan with all the artists over the next week so I would like to meet with you at some point."

I am so excited!

"I'm free whenever you need me Ellen. I'm actually going to take a little walk over there myself today."

"Well isn't that just dandy?" She has the sort of voice I would associate with arty gallery owner types. I always think they have such a sunny outlook on life. "I'll be in Glasgow after two this afternoon if you want to meet up then. The sooner the better."

"Okay, I'll meet you there. I'm going to spend some time in the park with my camera anyway."

"Fabulous, see you then darling."

We hang up and I hug my phone to my chest smiling with pride.

"I guess the call went well then since you look like the cat that got the cream," Steven smiles at me as he enters the office.

I throw my arms around his neck and kiss him. He seems startled by my forcefulness.

"Steven, right now I feel like this is where I was meant to be. You know at this particular point in my life things are amazing. Ellen is meeting me at the gallery later to discuss the layout for the pictures. They are giving my work the main exhibit space. Can you believe that? Me? The main exhibit space in the most beautiful art gallery. I'm stunned, I really am."

"I'm glad to see you're not lost for words though," he says with a cheeky smile.

I give him as stern a look as I can without laughing. "Okay, I know I'm rambling on but I'm not apologising for it. I'm so excited and I really hate to say this but I'm just a teeny tiny bit proud of myself."

"You have every right to be proud of yourself. It's about time you were a little selfish Gina. You do so much for everyone else. In my book pride is not a sin, let's leave that for the God-fearing folk."

I laugh at him, but he is right. I don't think it is a sin to feel good about something you have worked hard for. This is exactly what I need. A complete change from what I was doing before. I would love to be showing my photographs in galleries all over the world and this could be the stepping-stone to doing just that.

After walking Steven to work and having a little make-out session outside the front door, I make my way to the park. Hmm…yes, the park. The place that I used to love to be. I have been back a few times since the whole kidnapping and almost dying episode. On Nate's recommendation, and as soon as I was able, Steven took me back to where it all happened. At first, when Nate suggested it, I was filled with terror. The police tape was still on the bridge and I had a panic attack but thankfully Steven was there to help me through it. Over the last few weeks I have managed to walk here myself and since the bridge has been repaired you would never know that anything had happened.

What I haven't told anyone, even Steven, is that I have been documenting the progress of the bridge repairs by taking photos. I am going to take my final one today. I don't know what I am going to do with the photos, I didn't think that far ahead. It was just something I felt I had to do, self-therapy or something. I'm going to tell Nate at my session tomorrow. I think he will be proud of me. I do hope it can help heal me. I want to fall back in love with this dear green place.

The park is relatively quiet since it is mid-morning on a Monday. The only people here seem to be mothers with their pre-school children. It makes my heart pang slightly seeing them. I shake my head; there's plenty of time for that. I make my way towards the fountain in the park. I like to take pictures of moving water, there's something very serene about it. As the fountain comes into view, I can see that it is in full flow today. A couple sit in front of it talking. It looks romantic to me and I can feel my overactive sense of imagination kick into overdrive. I surreptitiously snap a couple of photos. Feeling a bit voyeuristic I zoom in for a close up and almost drop my camera when I see the couple stand up and the woman kiss the man on the cheek, her hand briefly caressing his face, before walking away.

As the man stoops to pick up his bag my worst fears are confirmed. The man I am looking at is my dad and that woman sure as hell isn't my mother.

CHAPTER 8

I ABRUPTLY TURN AND head towards some trees for cover. *What the hell is going on here?* My breathing is way too fast and my heart feels like it is going to burst out of my chest. I sit down under a tree and try to calm down. My mind is whirring with all sorts of scenarios, none of them good. I don't know what to do. Do I call my mum and tell her first or do I confront my dad and give him a chance to explain? How on earth would I even begin to explain this to my mum?

As my mind wars with itself I hear my phone herald a text message. Pulling it out of my bag I see it is from Ellen.

Going to be a little early Gina. Can we meet in half an hour instead of after 2?

A little early? It's only gone midday. Just as well

I'm already on my way there. I decide to put my dad off to one side for now and try to concentrate on myself. I'll deal with him later. I send Ellen a quick reply.

Fine by me I'll see you there.

The walk takes about ten minutes and by the time I get through the revolving door my nose and cheeks are freezing. The warmth inside the gallery is very inviting. As hard as I try to concentrate, I can't help picturing the image of my dad and that woman. I'm far too suspicious of everything now after all that has gone on in my life in the last few months. It is totally irrational, I know, but I can't help it. I think my session with Nate tomorrow is going to be a long one. Heading in through the main floor I make my way towards the stairs and down to the room that will display my work.

The room is huge and is accessed through a glass entrance. The walls are filled with what looks like African inspired tribal paintings. They are very vibrant and unusual. Ellen is already here and comes to greet me at the door.

"Ah Gina you're here. Come this way darling, this is my partner Simon Ponsonby, he co-owns the galleries with me."

She looks at him with a sweet smile on her face and I wonder if they are more than just business partners.

"Very nice to finally meet you Gina," Simon holds out his hand to shake mine.

He is English and has an air of sophistication about him. His blonde wavy hair and tweed jacket giving him a public-school boy look.

"And you. I'm really grateful to you both for this opportunity, thank you."

"I really loved your photos Gina, they are very dramatic. Those Aurora ones are by far my favourites and I have to say I am somewhat jealous. I've always wanted to see the northern lights. I tried once when I was in Shetland, but the weather had other ideas."

He laughs a hearty deep chuckle and I instantly like him. He reminds me of a younger version of my dad. The thought makes me feel a little uneasy and I decide to call him as soon as I am done here. I need to know what is going on.

"So Gina," Ellen interrupts my thoughts, "we are going to go through a wall and floor plan to sort out how we can best display your work. I have the other artists coming in over the next week or so but since you are the star attraction you get the full run through."

We spend the next hour drawing mock-ups on paper of what pictures will go where and what size they will be to best fit the space. Ellen and Simon have also asked for my permission to show them in Edinburgh when this exhibition is over and, they also want exclusive rights to sell my work for me. I am so blown away by everything, my luck has taken a complete 360-degree turn in the last few days and I'm reeling. We say our goodbyes at the front entrance and as Ellen and Simon leave, I see them holding hands and realise I was right, they *are* more than just business partners.

I make my way back home and decide to stop in and see Steven. As I approach his office, I see my dad's mystery woman exiting the building. Seriously? I can feel my blood boiling. In my mind I am trying to rationalise things, but my heart has always been stronger and right now my heart feels like it has sunk into my stomach. Something doesn't feel right. I watch her as she walks away from the entrance and thank God she is going in the opposite direction to me. I take the stairs two at a time and burst through Steven's door looking like a woman possessed. Cerys is sitting at her desk, but Steven is nowhere to be seen.

"Well that's one way to make an entrance. Are you okay Gina?"

I feel a little silly now and I don't really know what I was intending to say to Steven if he had been here.

"Yeah, eh... is Steven around?"

"He's just out of a meeting but he went up to see Nate. Are you sure you're okay? You look a little pale. Would you like a coffee?"

"Yes please."

As she gets up to pour two coffees from the pot, I decide to confront her instead. "Who was he meeting with Cerys?"

She doesn't turn to look at me when she answers. "Uhm…I think she was a new client."

She is lying I know it. She can't even look me in the eye.

"What does she want Steven to do?"

"I don't actually know he left as soon as she was gone. So, I hear you've had some good news about your photos." She smiles sweetly trying to change the subject.

I shake my head at her. "Uh uh Cerys, tell me what you know."

She shakes her head and lowers her gaze in defeat. "Okay, I honestly don't know that much though."

"I promise I won't say anything I just want to know who that woman was. I saw her in the park with my dad right before I went to meet the gallery owner and then I saw her leaving here."

Cerys leads me into the meeting room and closes the door behind her. We both take a seat.

"So?" I say impatiently.

"Okay, I know her name but that's all I can tell you. Steven and your dad had a meeting with her before they went to play golf the other day. It was the weekend, I wasn't supposed to be working but he asked

67

me to come in to do tea and coffee. I was a bit pissed off at him actually because it was a last minute thing. Totally ruined my shopping plans for the day."

She opens the diary she has in front of her and points to a name on the page for today.

"Andrea Marshall. I recognise that name from somewhere." I wrack my brain to try and remember where I have seen or heard the name but it's useless.

"Now I know as much as you Gina. I really don't think there is anything sinister going on though, you really shouldn't worry yourself for no reason."

Of course, I know deep down she is right but after recent events I can't help but have a sneaking suspicion that everyone is hiding something from me. It's pissing me off to be honest. It seems that all I do these days is stress over stupid insignificant things. That saying making a mountain out of a molehill definitely applies to me.

"I'm sorry Cerys. I'm goddamn pathetic I know."

She shakes her head. "No, you're not Gina. You're one of the strongest people I know. I mean look at what's happened to you and you're still here. I swear you have balls girl."

I actually snort a laugh at her.

"Well on that note I'll leave you to it. I think Mr Parker has some explaining to do. I'll deal with him when he gets home."

"Okay honey sorry I couldn't help." Cerys blows me a kiss as I leave and I glimpse the tiniest look of relief on her face.

There is no way am I being kept in the dark again. I turn abruptly and slam my palms down on the table. The noise is so loud I think they will have heard it upstairs and I have to say it stings my skin slightly. For the first time since I've known her, Cerys looks lost for words.

"Talk now Cerys. And no lies this time."

CHAPTER 9

STEVEN'S EXPLANATION REGARDING THE mysterious Andrea Marshall was as convincing as hell. She is a friend and former colleague of my dad's. That much I know is true and I now know where I recognised her name from. She was a lecturer in Physics at Glasgow Uni when I was there. Steven is supposedly helping her with her property sale and it was all very innocent according to him.

That story seems plausible, but I'd still like know my dad's take on Andrea. That interaction in the park looked far too intimate to me and less than innocent.

What I didn't expect was for Cerys to spill the beans about everything Steven has been doing. Three days later, I'm still finding it hard to keep it to myself and not let on that I have rumbled what should have been an amazing secret. Poor Cerys, I really hope she forgives me. I didn't realise how intimidating I had been towards her. Seeing my dad in that compromising situation has seriously messed with my head.

I'm meeting up with Charlie and Nikki today to show them the flat. I'm sure Nikki will love it, what twenty-six year-old wouldn't love living right in the heart of this beautiful vibrant city?

"So what time are you meeting Charlie then?" Steven asks from his seat at the breakfast table.

He is sitting munching on some toast with three A3 size pieces of paper spread out in front of him.

"About noon. We are going to go for lunch and giving Nikki a guided tour of the city. She also has her interview today."

Steven looks at his watch and then at me. His right eyebrow raises slightly and his eyes glint with that look I have come to know very well.

"For goodness sake man you're wearing me out here."

His smile widens and a mock look of innocence befalls his face.

"I am sure I do not know what you are insinuating my dear."

"Sorry honey but I have a date with two beautiful ladies." I smile my sweetest, innocent smile but my comment only serves to make his smile even cheekier.

All I can do is hold up my hands in defeat and shake

my head.

***

My taxi arrives at Central Station within five minutes which is quick considering the amount of road works going on in the city right now. I am about to pay the driver when he pipes up, "Its awright hen, wee Steven's got an account with us."

I smile and wonder to myself how he knows who I am and that I am in any way associated with Steven. Then I remember how convenient it was that I got a black cab as soon as I was out of the apartment building. He just happened to be driving by at the exact time I was leaving. I really wish Steven would just run things by me and maybe ask if I need a taxi instead of being so cloak and dagger about it. I know his heart is in the right place and that he wants to protect me, but he is going about it all wrong. I feel this is yet another little discussion I am going to have to have with him when I get home.

As I enter the station at the Gordon Street entrance, I can already see Charlie standing with one hand on Georgie's pram, holding a Starbucks in the other. The young lady standing next to her is a taller, slimmer version of Charlie with the same flawless skin and beautiful blonde hair. Charlie spots me instantly and throws me a cute wink.

"Well hello my lovely," Charlie says as I near them.

"Hello to you too my dear, and hello you very grown up little Nikki."

Nikki smiles a shy but very beautiful smile and immediately holds out her hand to shake mine. I take it and turn to Charlie.

"I see she got all the manners, what happened to you?"

She responds with a laugh and a punch to my arm. "Shut it bitch-face."

"It's lovely to see you again Gina," Nikki's accent is much stronger South African compared to her sister, but I do note the tiniest hint of Scots in there. Charlie has a more prominent Scottish twang to hers.

Charlie was born in Glasgow but moved to South Africa when she was four years old with her parents when her dad took a job at the British High Commission. Nikki was born in South Africa and didn't follow in her sister's footsteps by studying abroad. Charlie said she wanted to come back to her roots in Scotland, so as soon as she was able to, she did and hasn't looked back since.

Now Nikki is coming to live in Glasgow and I can tell from the gleam in Charlie's eyes when she looks at her little sister that this is the icing on the cake for her.

"It's so great to see you again honey. I'm sure you're

going to absolutely love living here. I can't wait to show you the flat. Did Charlie tell you about it?"

"She did and I can't thank you enough for your help. It makes the move easier for me. It also makes mum and dad happier knowing I'll get settled quickly. They worry too much, I think."

Charlie snorts, "Yeah we can't have the blue eyed girl being out of sorts on her big move. You're twenty-six for god sake, I was only nineteen."

I know Charlie is only trying to wind her sister up, but Nikki looks like she is going to burst in to tears.

"Whatever Charlie," Nikki gives her sister a hurt look and walks away towards the Starbucks kiosk.

Charlie frowns. "Well I don't know what's crawled up her arse but that was very unlike her. To be honest I'm a little worried about her. She's not her usual happy go lucky self. I don't know if it's the move but something's not right."

"I'm sure she'll be fine. It's all very new. I mean she's lived with your parents all her life so this has to be quite daunting for her. She'll be nervous about her interview today as well."

"I hope that's all it is Gina. She has such a good nature normally, we need to try and find it today."

I watch Nikki as she pays for her coffee. She looks frail from where we are standing, and she never makes eye contact with the male barista. It's strange but it looks like she is scared of him or something. She takes her coffee from the girl at the end and gives her a smile. I look at Charlie and I realise she noticed it too. Her brows are furrowed and she has that certain mother hen look about her.

"I swear to God Gina if someone has hurt my baby sister, I am going to have his balls on a skewer."

Yes, she definitely saw what I saw.

"I think the sooner she moves here the better. I can see this is going to be eating you up until she's safely under your wing."

"That's the thing Gina, she's just so closed off. When I met her and mum at the airport she wouldn't even hug me. She shook my hand. Since when does your sister shake your hand? She hasn't even made any attempt to bond with Georgie. All she does is sit with earphones in reading books."

I feel for Charlie. She was so excited about seeing her wee sister again, but it seems all it is doing is causing her stress.

"Have you spoken to your mum about it?"

"Yeah she says it's a phase. I think mum's head is elsewhere right now trying to get ready for the move so I don 't think she's seeing the bigger picture. Twenty-six year-old grown women don't go through phases."

"Go easy on her honey, if you go at it all guns

75

blazing, she'll never tell you anything."

Charlie smiles. "You know me Gina, I am the epitome of discretion."

I smile at her and shake my head. Discrete my arse.

"So, how's my favourite little lady doing?" I place a light kiss on Georgie's tiny little hand and she stirs ever so slightly but continues in her blissful slumber.

"Having a great time now grandma is here. Well I'm having a great time now grandma is here. I've actually been able to have a shower that lasts longer than a minute."

Nikki joins us again and looks a little more composed. She gives Charlie a shy little smile and Charlie smiles back. The unspoken truce between them is very noticeable. I think they'll be fine.

***

Lunch has been a subdued affair so far. I am starting to get the feeling that Charlie is right and that there is something wrong with Nikki. I don't know her at all really but there is something about a person's mannerisms and body language that speaks louder than words ever can. As we finish our desserts, Georgie lets out a high-pitched squeal and proceeds to bring the house down.

"Well it was too good to be true that mummy might have gotten through a full meal, but you almost did it wee one." Charlie stands and takes the brake off the pram. "I think madam needs changed. I'll be back shortly girls."

As soon as she is far enough away, I take the opportunity to find out what's eating Nikki. I put my hand on hers.

"Penny for your thoughts honey."

She shakes her head. "I'm fine Gina. I'm..." She looks down at the table and starts to cry.

"Nikki tell me what's wrong sweetheart. I promise I won't say anything to Charlie if you don't want me to."

It takes her a few moments to compose herself.

"I feel so stupid Gina. I'm not a pushover but this guy is..." She trails off as she sees Charlie coming back towards us, Georgie in one arm and pram handle in the other. I shift my attention to watching my friend and beaming over how brilliant a mother she is. She will be able to help her little sister with whatever is going on.

"Talk to your sister Nikki," I whisper.

Nikki gives me a small smile. I don't know whether she will say anything to Charlie or not, but I think this is one for them to work out alone. I don't know Nikki well enough to be able to give her advice.

"Jesus Christ it's like a wake at this table. Who died?"

I can't help myself but laugh at her. "You know if you'd said that to me a few months ago I would have been a mess on the floor."

Charlie nods. "Yeah honey you dodged a bullet with that one I'll tell you. Now come on you two get some smiles on those faces."

Nikki gives her sister a small smile.

"So Gina anything planned for your birthday yet? I was going to suggest going for a spa day. My poor aching body needs it."

I smile at her. I know she's leading me up the garden path here because Cerys has already told me everything. Although I have yet to speak to my dad about what was going on between him and Andrea. I honestly hope Steven isn't covering for him if he's been up to no good. Considering what I've been through it would be the biggest betrayal imaginable.

Steven has organised a surprise birthday party for me and Charlie knows it. I'm rather nervous about it because I'm not one for being the centre of attention. And herein lies my problem with having to know everything. Now I have time to stew over it and get myself worked up into a state instead of just enjoying it when it is thrust upon me.

"That sounds good to me honey." I smile at her.

We finish up our desserts and make our way to the apartment, which is only a few minutes' walk away. I watch Nikki as we walk and notice that she is admiring the buildings around us and every so often I catch a glimpse of a smile on her lips. I get the feeling this move is going to do her the world of good.

CHAPTER 10

THE CITY SKY HAS turned a mucky grey colour and, as I stare out the window of the beautiful home I will never live in, I am struck by just how much has changed for me in such a short period of time. I wonder how the hell I am still functioning given the fact that I almost died and found out my marriage was a sham in the space of a few weeks. I am glad I had Steven to help me through everything but a part of me, a horrible, tiny niggly part of me, wonders if those things would have happened if I had never met him. I shake my head. It's a part of me I would like to pretend doesn't exist.

I said goodbye to Charlie and Nikki a little over an hour ago and, as yet, I have not been able to leave. I don't know what is keeping me here. I have never spent a night in this flat and I don't have any sentimental connection to it. Nikki fell in love with the place as soon as she stepped over the threshold. Her face lit up and she looked genuinely happy. I'm pleased that I can do something to help her, she seems so down; now I know it has something to do with a guy, I am worried about her. I hope she can confide in Charlie. I have found out the hard way that keeping things to yourself and trying to deal with problems on your own just doesn't work. My phone pings.

Hey gorgeous. How about going out for an Indian tonight? xx

Ugh. I couldn't stomach any more heavy food after our Chinese lunch today.

Sorry honey we had Chinese today so I don't want anything too heavy. x

I reply and am greeted with a reply almost straight away.

You're still at the apartment. Stay there I'll be 10 mins. xx

For a second, I wonder how he knows but then I remember he has my phone tracked. I feel safe knowing that he knows where I am but sometimes I worry that it's unhealthy. I know he blames himself and I can't change that, no matter how much I try.

***

The buzz of the intercom piercing through the silence makes me jump. I put my hand to my chest and feel my heart beat fast. I know it is Steven, but the slightest thing makes me jump these days. A few days ago, I was getting food out of the fridge to make a salad and when I shut the door Steven was standing right there. The poor guy got whacked with a cucumber and I felt so stupid.

I buzz him in and open the front door. I can hear him whistling to himself as he climbs the stairs. His good mood is catchy and I find myself smiling. As he rounds the stairs, I feel a flutter in my belly. It doesn't matter how many times I see that beautiful face it still gives me butterflies. I feel like a silly schoolgirl, but it is nice, and I haven't felt that way since I *was* a schoolgirl.

"Well hello handsome." I am rewarded with that sexy wink.

Steven rushes towards me and almost lifts me off the floor. Swooping me back he leans in and kisses me, letting his lips linger a fraction longer that he needs to.

"Hello gorgeous," he whispers against my lips. His breath is hot and minty.

"Mmmm," I murmur.

"Is everyone gone?"

"Yes, why?"

"I have a surprise."

Steven pulls his phone out of his pocket and sends a quick text then ushers me inside. This is the first time he has been here but the nod of his head and the smile on his face says he approves.

"You picked a good one here Gina. This place is lovely. I hope Nikki realises how lucky she is to get to stay here."

"She does. She is absolutely delighted. In fact, it was the first time she's actually smiled since she got here that didn't look forced."

His brows furrow slightly. "What's up with her?"

"I don't know but from what she told me it has something to do with a guy."

"Charlie won't be happy if someone has hurt her baby sister will she?"

"She won't talk to Charlie, but Charlie knows there's something wrong. Unless she opens up there's not a lot Charlie can do."

Steven throws me a raised eyebrow, obviously referring to my unwillingness to open up.

"Don't you start pal. I seem to recall that you are just as guilty of holding onto too much."

He is about to speak but is stopped by the intercom buzzing. "That'll be your surprise. Stay here gorgeous." He plants a swift kiss on my lips and disappears down the hall and out the door.

I am filled with a sense of contentment and I love

it. When I hear the door open, I turn and find Steven walking towards me with a picnic basket over his arm and a bottle of Bollinger in the other hand. This man never ceases to amaze me. It is becoming more and more apparent that he is always thinking of me and trying to find new ways to make me happy.

"Mr Parker is there nothing you can do wrong?"

His smile falters a little at my words and I know exactly what is going on in that head of his.

"Right what do you have in there you master of surprise?" I'm relieved when his smile returns.

"You'll see," he says as he opens the basket and pulls out a red tartan blanket.

He shakes it out and lays it on the floor in the huge living room. I smile as I watch him busy himself emptying the basket. I laugh when he lifts out the last item. A battery-operated candle. He switches it on and places it in the middle of all the food. It runs through the spectrum of colours and since it is starting to darken outside the light is welcome.

"Let's eat gorgeous." Steven holds out his hand to me and I take it and sit beside him. Lifting a teeny tiny sandwich, he gestures to me to open my mouth. I oblige and let him feed me, which I have to say feels a little strange. The filling is delicate and melt in the mouth.

The array of food, from the goat cheese and onion

tarts to the mini cake pops decorated with tiny love hearts, is sublime and in no time, we are finished.

As we sit against the wall drinking champagne and chatting, I take stock of just how lucky I am. I have a wonderful man by my side and an amazing family. Not to forget my crazy best friend. I feel blessed after everything that has happened to me. Every day my positivity is growing.

"So, I haven't asked yet, where was Nikki interviewing today?" Steven asks looking genuinely interested.

"Ehm… I don't remember the name of the place. It's over at the Broomielaw. Secure Soft or something like that I think."

"SecuriSoft? Hmm that's interesting."

I shoot him a quizzical look. "Why? And if you say you own it, I'll eat my hat."

"Ha, well I don't own it, so your hat is safe. Dan King is a friend of mine. Well, I say friend, more a business acquaintance who is like a friend."

I know Steven doesn't class many people as friends, although they would beg to differ, so for him to even mention the word I can tell this guy is probably more than a business acquaintance.

"Really? I think she'll do well. Charlie says her current boss has given her a good reference. She's a very clever girl you know. She has helped design some fantastic security software that has been used in quite a few government buildings in South Africa."

"Well she will fit in very well with Dan. He's always on the lookout for new talent. His company has one of the best in-house training schemes I've ever come across. He's a good boss too. His employees all love him."

I smile at him. "Your employees love you too you know."

"What can I say? I'm a lovable guy," he says and throws me a wink.

I pick up a piece of crusty bread and throw it at him. "Big head."

I am taken aback when he picks up a cream cake and launches himself at me, pinning me to the floor and holding the cake above me.

"Beg me not to," he says, his voice rough and husky.

I shake my head but can't help the smile that spreads over my face.

"You asked for it," he says.

Before I can protest, he swipes cream on to my nose. I squeal and try to push him off me but he's a solid mass of muscle and stays stock-still.

"Eeww… get that off me. It'll get me all sticky."

Steven gives me a wicked smile and proceeds to lick the cream off my nose. When it is gone, he leans in close and whispers in my ear, "I'll give you sticky."

His words make my insides somersault

"I have something for you," he says reaching in to his trouser pocket.

When he pulls out a piece of black rope I gasp. It's the same rope I saw in the stage show at Black.

"Hmm... you remembered," I breathe as goose bumps form on my skin.

"I always listen Gina, anything you want I'll give you." He takes the end of the rope and runs it over my lips. "What should I do with this Gina?"

How can I answer that? I don't do sexy talk; it embarrasses me.

"Tell me Gina," Steven whispers right next to my ear.

"I can't."

"Close your eyes and tell me."

I do as he says, and I start to feel a little less shy. "I want you to tie my hands."

"And then what should I do?"

I squirm a little under him. "Mmm...I want you to tie my hands and fuck me. Take what you want from me."

I open my eyes and am faced with the blazing heat of Steven's gaze. He stands up and pulls me to my feet. He guides me towards the island in the middle of the kitchen and places the rope on the work surface. I am very quickly relieved of all my clothes until I am standing in front of him completely naked. I watch as he picks up the rope and throws it over the empty island utensil rack above my head. He lifts me onto the island. The chill under my bum makes me squeal. He lifts my knickers off the floor and pulls my wrists together. I am a little confused when he puts the panties round my wrists.

"Stops rope burns," he says obviously catching my confused look.

I watch as he sets about tying a loose end of the rope round my wrists in a knot any boy scout would be proud of. As he pulls on the other end my hands are raised above my head until they are suspended in mid-air.

"Does that feel okay?" He asks as he ties it off so that I can't pull them down.

My body is tingling with delicious anticipation.

"Yes, it's fine." I manage to say and then watch mesmerised as he strips off his own clothes, his muscles rippling and setting off sparks in my body.

He has his erection sheathed in a condom in double quick time and jumps up onto the island and kneels beside me, pulling my legs round so that I am sitting on his thighs. For a second, I feel weightless and its altogether amazingly freeing and truly terrifying. I'm a little worried that this rack is not going to hold my weight and that very soon we'll be sitting here naked and covered in plaster when it gives way.

"You'll be fine," says Steven as if sensing my fears.

He has one hand at my back and runs his other hand down my face, splaying his fingers as he moves it down the centre of my torso. I arch my back, bucking my pelvis towards him. He pushes my breast up slightly and takes my hard nipple in his mouth, sucking it in and nipping it with his teeth. As he moves his hand towards my swollen sex I can no longer control my wanton body. My hips move involuntarily and as soon as his fingers skim my clit I am done for. My body is a quivering mess and the fact that I am trussed up and can't move my arms makes the feeling all the more intense.

I have no time to recover as Steven lifts my hips and slides inside me. The angle I am sitting at helps him hit that sweet spot straight away and he doesn't hang around. As we move in unison it takes us both no time at all to reach orgasm and as he comes his hips buck against my clit sending me over the edge. We writhe against each other until we are both wrung out. Steven reaches above my head and unties the rope allowing my arms to fall. The rush of blood back into them gives me pins and needles. He rubs my arms to get the feeling back in them.

"You ok?" He asks.

"Very," I say with a smile.

He unties the rope from my wrists and hands me my knickers. I rub my wrists and can't keep the smile off my face. I burst into a hysterical laugh. "Poor Nikki. I'm going to have to deep clean this kitchen before I hand her the keys."

Steven laughs. "Yeah, way to christen a house Gina you naughty girl. I can't believe you made me do that."

"Oh yeah, blame me. I can't help it if you are too persuasive. Anyway, I wasn't the one who came prepared with bondage paraphernalia," I laugh at him.

We tidy up the picnic basket and head for the door.

"Steven," I whisper at his back.

He turns to me.

"What?"

"Did you remember the rope?" I smile at him.

He puts his hand in my hair and pulls it slightly kissing me roughly. "Yes," he whispers against my lips. "And I have plenty more where that came from."

CHAPTER 11

I AM EXTREMELY EXCITED today. Charlie and Mark are going to a family wedding tomorrow and they have asked if Steven and I will babysit Georgie overnight. Her mum and sister fly back to South Africa today so I'm the next best thing apparently. Of course I said yes without hesitation, however, in my haste I didn't think to run it by Steven so now I am going to his office to do just that.

I have noticed over the last few weeks that the trees and shrubs are starting to look a bit greener and the weather is taking on a more spring like quality. The days are getting longer too and it is making me long for summer. Okay, summer in Scotland isn't like summer in other parts of the world but we are a hardy bunch. As soon as it hits March and the temperature goes above 10°C all hell breaks loose. The men strip to the waist showing off their pasty white bodies and the women wear as little clothing as is legal. Since glorious sunny weather is a phenomenon in Glasgow this behaviour is not too common, thank goodness.

As I reach the foot of the stairs to Steven's office building, I am overcome by a woozy, nauseous sensation. Grabbing the railing next to the stairs I wait until it passes. I put it down to low blood sugar since I haven't eaten anything yet and it is already 11am. The building is busy this morning and I pass a multitude of people coming and going as I make my way upstairs. Opening Steven's door, I find Cerys at her desk obviously deep in frustrated concentration judging by the frown on her face.

"Morning Cerys."

She looks up. "Good morning Gina. Steven is through in the meeting room, I'll let him know you're here?"

"I'll just go on through if that's okay. I'll surprise him."

Cerys nods and returns her attention to the computer screen. I make my way along the short corridor to the room at the end and find the door open. I stand and stare, mesmerised.

Steven is pacing in front of a white projector screen talking and gesturing with his hands. There is nothing on the screen and no one else in the room but his presence is mighty. If he can command an empty room like this, I would love to see how he handles a room full of people. I can picture him giving a speech or a presentation and every set of eyes in the room being transfixed on him. I breathe out a loving sigh and it startles him. He turns and looks at me and the most beautiful sincere smile crosses his face.

"Hey gorgeous. Enjoying yourself there?"

"Absolutely. What are you up to?"

"I've a meeting with a building company on Monday. I've been toying with the idea of house building for a while now and I think the time is right."

"Well you did have the house on Harris built so there's nothing to stop you. That is one stunning building."

Steven smiles, stalking me from the other side of the table before catching me around the waist.

"You're a special woman Gina do you know that? I have to pinch myself sometimes to believe that you're real. I still find it hard to grasp that people actually believe in me. Support and encouragement weren't exactly overflowing when I was growing up."

My heart is about to burst. I can't offer anything in reply. Stroking his stubbly jawline, I place a soft lingering kiss on his lips.

"So, to what do I owe the pleasure of this little visit?"

"Charlie called me this morning and asked if we could babysit Georgie at the weekend. They have a family wedding to go to and she thinks Georgie is too young. To be honest I think she just doesn't want all of Marks family pawing all over her and I know she hasn't been out since Georgie was born so she probably wants to let her hair down," I take a breath and look at Steven who is smiling from ear to ear.

"What?"

"You know I would love to have her stay over Gina, you don't need to justify it."

I need to give this guy more credit "Sorry. I felt bad for agreeing before I had run it by you, I mean it's your house after all."

Steven shakes his head and frowns at me.

"Gina, you live there too. It's *our* home."

"But I haven't contributed anything to it, so I don't feel that's fair."

"It's bricks and mortar. You've made it feel like a home since you've been there." He gives me a wink. "So, when does the princess arrive then?"

"Tomorrow morning. The wedding is at two, but they want to get there early. I won't even go into the conversation I had with Charlie about the baby's milk, you really don't want to know."

I smile remembering the words *I've been pumping for Scotland* sending me into hysterics to the point where I couldn't see for the tears.

"I know Charlie, and no I don't want to know."

"Wise decision. So are you going to be much longer here?" I sit up on the table in front of him. "I thought we could take a walk over to the art gallery and I can show you where my photos will be exhibited. Ellen emailed this morning to say that the prints have arrived at Kelvingrove and they look absolutely amazing. I'm so excited Steven I feel like this is going to be the start of something fantastic."

"That sounds like a great idea. I was going to let Cerys go early anyway, she asked this morning and I've been keeping her in suspense all morning." He smiles slyly. "Got to keep my staff on their toes, can't have them thinking I'm a pushover."

I shake my head. "You, a pushover, nah, you're tough as nails."

I push his shoulder and he swiftly grabs my wrists wrapping my arms behind my back and holding them both with one hand. My breath catches in my throat as I remember being bound by the velvet rope in my apartment. He trails his finger down my neck and my body arches in response. Splaying his hand as it reaches my sternum, he kisses my neck and a quiet moan escapes my lips.

"Oh shit sorry."

Steven and I both jump at the intrusive voice but

even though I am as embarrassed as all hell, it's not a patch on the look on Cerys' face. I can't help myself as I hit a fit of the giggles. It's not long before she is laughing too. Steven merely shakes his head.

"Yes, Cerys, what can I do for you?" He tries to make himself sound all stern and important but the smile on his face gives him away.

"I've finished typing up the reports you gave me and all the filing is done. I was just wondering if there is anything else you need me to do today or…" She trails off and looks at Steven with expectant eyes.

"Yes, there are five sets of drawings and building warrant applications on my desk that need to be typed up and emailed by the end of business today."

Poor Cerys looks deflated. "Oh okay. I'll get on to them right now."

As she walks away from the door I shake my head at Steven who is gleeful in his evilness.

"You are so bad Steven. You need to tell her she can go."

"I will, but I'm enjoying this too much. Let me just get tidied up here and we can get the weekend started, I'm quite looking forward to it now."

I watch as he moves fluidly around the room shutting everything down and I know if I were a cartoon character, I would have those giant sparkling eyes and love hearts floating out the top of my head. It still surprises me to realise how much in love and lust I am with this man.

"Right gorgeous, ready?" Steven breaks my little bubble of love and holds his hand out to me.

I take it and jump down from the table.

"Absolutely handsome."

We find Cerys sitting at her desk wading through a stack of files with a puzzled look on her face. Cocking her head to one side a smile gradually emerges as she looks at Steven.

"You fucking shithead Steven, these are all done," she laughs.

"Got to keep you on your toes Cerys. I can't have you telling everyone I'm an amazing boss. I have a reputation to keep you know."

Cerys sticks her tongue out at him. "How do you put up with him Gina?"

"Watch it or I'll lock you in for the weekend."

She smiles and shakes her head in defeat.

"Right we are off, have a nice weekend," Steven winks at her and takes my hand again.

"Yeah, you too."

As we leave, I look back at Cerys and she smiles at me then sticks her fingers up at Steven's back. I giggle and blow her a kiss.

The air outside has turned damp and a fine drizzle has left beads on the cars parked outside the building.

We make our way across the park towards the art gallery chatting about everything and nothing. I love the fact that Steven is genuinely interested in what I have to say, and the feeling is mutual. I am still in awe of how much he has achieved at such a young age. The thought brings to mind an idea I had floated in my mind a while ago, before I found out that my husband had been a lying son of a bitch.

"Hey, can I run something by you?" I ask as we reach the steps of the art gallery.

Steven cocks his head and smiles.

"Sure babe, what's up?"

"Well, you know that I still have some of the money left from Aiden's life insurance?"

He narrows his eyes at the mention of the name. I know he hates what happened to me, but I have made my peace with it. It was one of those things that show the true complexities of human emotion. As my mum says, the heart wants what it wants and nothing I could have done could stop Aiden from finding someone else. The more time I spend with Steven the more I realise that Aiden and I really weren't suited. It's a shame that it took him losing his life for me to realise it. It still hurts to know that he couldn't talk to me and tell me that he was in love with someone else. Sure, I would have been devastated but I know I wouldn't have stood in his way. But then I probably wouldn't have met Steven, I selfishly think to myself. It's true, I would never have had grief counselling but that's not all Nate does. I may have needed him anyway. Maybe we were just meant to be. Like Steven said.

"I was thinking…"

"Oh God whenever a sentence starts with *I was thinking* it can't be good. I get that from clients all the time when I'm almost finished their plans and they decide to change something, that's what they always say."

"No nothing bad can come from this I promise, it's all good."

"Do proceed then," Steven gestures with his hand.

"So, I have just short of four hundred thousand pounds left after paying for my apartment and having basically lived off what I had for the last six months."

Steven watches me intently, taking in absolutely everything I am saying. It makes me smile.

"Well, I was trying to work out how best to use it. I really don't want it: it's tainted. You know it was never intended for me but if I put it to a good cause it might make me feel better."

"What a fantastic idea. What did you have in mind? Do you want to give it to a charity or something?"

"I did consider that, but I would love to put it to something I can be involved in. I would love to do something myself and maybe get some investment from, say, a local businessperson. Would you know of anyone I could ask?"

Steven's eyes crinkle at the corners as a huge smile crosses his face.

"Hmm…let me think about that." He rubs his stubbly chin. "No, sorry, I don't know anyone like that." He is laughing too hard at his own joke and I can't help but join in.

"Oh no, what is a girl to do?" I put the back of my hand to my forehead, a damsel in distress.

What Steven decides to do next has me almost pissing myself laughing, literally. He turns to me and sticks out his chest, holding his right arm out in front of him.

"Aha fair maiden, tis' I Sir Stevealot, I am your knight in shining armour. I shall bequeath to you six hundred thousand golden coins to make your dream come true."

I stop laughing as I realise he is not kidding. A million pounds, this is too amazing for words. I launch myself at him and hug him with all my might.

"You are an amazing man Steven Parker. Don't ever forget that."

He looks into my eyes. "It's your idea, I'm just supporting it. I have some people you can talk to about starting up a charity, they'll give you some really good advice and training."

"I want you to be involved too though. I don't want you being a silent benefactor. I would love this to be something we do together, you know, as a couple."

Steven closes his eyes and his brow creases slightly.

"Are you okay?"

He opens his eyes and shakes his head.

"God Gina, you have no idea what those words do to me."

"So is that a yes then?"

"Of course it is you wonderful woman." He smiles as he lifts me off my feet, kissing me hard. "We can get the ball rolling on Monday. I'll take the day off and we can brainstorm."

His genuine enthusiasm is infectious, and we enter the art gallery grinning like idiots.

CHAPTER 12

"GUYS SHE WILL BE fine. Please go and enjoy your freedom."

Charlie is hesitant and I can see her lip start to tremble. "Oh my God Georgie, what have you bloody done to me?" She whispers at the sleeping baby.

I try my best to console her. "Look, you know you can pick her up any time you want. Go and enjoy the wedding and if you really can't stand to be away from her overnight, we can bring her to you, and we can take you all home. Now please don't ruin that smoking hot look you have going on there. Snot on the face is not very sexy."

Charlie laughs in spite of her emotional dilemma. "Okay let's get out of here Mark before I change my mind."

She places a kiss on Georgie's head and grabs

Mark's arm. As we reach the door, she hesitates so I give her a little push.

"Beat it or I won't babysit again."

Charlie gives me a smile and they head downstairs.

"Thanks Gina," Mark shouts and I close the door after them.

I have to admit I am a little overwhelmed. I lean back against the door and close my eyes.

"Hey you okay?" Steven's voice breaks the silence. "You look like you're getting ready to go into battle or something."

I shake my head.

"I'm fine, honestly, I think Charlie's anxiety has rubbed off on me. I'm excited to be looking after Georgie but I'm apprehensive too. What if she doesn't like us or we do something wrong with her or..."

"Sshh," Steven puts his finger on my lips. "We'll be fine. You know Charlie wouldn't have trusted us with her if she thought otherwise. I imagine it's hard for any parent to leave their child for the first time."

A dark look momentarily crosses Stevens face. The pain of his childhood coming to the fore, once again, but no sooner has it appeared than it is gone. He shakes his head and smiles.

"So, do you want to go and get some lunch?"

"Sounds good to me. Where to?" I ask knowing he'll find us somewhere excellent to eat.

"I know a great little bistro near the University. The weather is nice enough to walk."

"Let's go then. We just need to try and figure out this pram. I think you need an actual degree to even get it open."

I press a button on the contraption sitting in the hallway and one of the wheels falls off. We both look at each other and burst into hysterics.

***

Kelvingrove Park is busy this afternoon. We finally managed to conquer the pram after about 10 minutes of wrestling with it, laughing and swearing. Steven is pushing Georgie's pram with me on his arm, domestic bliss. I imagine anyone looking at us would think we were proud new parents out for a walk with our baby and the thought makes me feel a bit sad. I push the thought down as deep as it will go. Is it silly to pine over something you never actually had?

Steven's ringtone pierces the air and I jump. "Sorry babe I need to take this," he says letting me take the pram.

"I'll go and sit over there." I point to the play area where a bunch of kids are running around like lunatics and some mothers are sitting talking. He nods and answers his phone. I take a seat and put the brake on the pram. My phone pings and I check the message.

It's from Charlie.

Hey. Arrived safely. Missing my girl. x

Poor Charlie. This little girl really has had a huge effect on her and as I look at her asleep in her pram I know why.

Good enjoy yourselves. We are out having a wee walk. Baby is fine. Xx

A shadow looms over me and looking up I see a young woman with long dark auburn hair and striking amber eyes.

"Can I help you?"

She averts her gaze and looks behind me. I turn my head in the direction of her stare and see that she is looking at Steven who has his back to us, still on the phone. When I look back at her I notice that she is scowling at his back.

"Can I help you?" I ask again.

I'm starting to get a little annoyed. Again, she ignores my question and I am about to get up and walk away when Steven appears on the other side of me.

"Let's go," he says, his tone short and clipped and grabs my arm so hard that it hurts slightly.

"Hey, that hurt."

He lets go and I notice that he and the auburn haired woman are locked in some sort of weird staring competition. I look from one to the other and it becomes apparent that they know each other.

I am about to ask what is going on when the woman speaks.

"Well, isn't this a blast from the past. How are you Steven?"

"What the hell are you doing here Leah?"

Leah? The ex-fiancée? My body turns cold and I feel instantly thankful to be seated although I feel at a bit of a disadvantage at this low level.

"It's a free country Steven. Last time I checked, this park doesn't belong to you."

"Gina, please can we go?" He asks.

I stand and take the brake off the pram. As we are about to walk away one of the children who had been playing on the swings runs over and calls Leah mummy. Steven turns his back and is already walking away. I catch up with him and then the shit hits the fan.

"Don't fucking walk away from me Steven!" Leah shouts at our backs. "He's yours."

Steven stops dead. My grip on the pram handle tightens and I can feel my heartbeat start to rise. She is standing with her hand on her hip and a sneer on her face while her poor little boy looks like he has seen a ghost. I get the feeling this is the first he has heard of this. The crowd around us seems to have stopped in time. Every pair of eyes are on the spectacle happening in front of them and I can feel the redness rising up from my neck. Steven looks like he is about to pop a vein and I know I'm going to have to get him out of here as soon as I can.

"Do you have a business card?" I ask him as quietly as I can.

"Why the fuck are you asking me that?" He says through gritted teeth.

"I know what I'm doing and rather than escalate this situation further and risk you getting jailed just give me a card if you have one. I'd like to get out of here and get this little girl back to her parents in one piece."

My voice is shaking slightly. Steven relents and pulls a business card from his inside pocket. I take it and give him a nod.

"Take Georgie out of here I won't be long." Handing the pram over to him I watch as he walks away.

Turning my attention back to Leah, I see that she is still smirking. Her son is standing beside her holding her hand and looking like a little lost soul.

"You playing messenger for him? Can the weirdo not even talk to me himself? You must feel so proud to be with someone who can't acknowledge his responsibilities. Your kid better get used to not having a daddy when he fucks off and leaves you."

"I would advise you to contact a solicitor Leah. These are Steven's contact details. Please do this properly, don't make a fool of yourself."

"Yeah okay, he's always been like that..."

I cut her off. "If what you say is true, I have no doubt Steven will step up. You can't drop a bombshell like that and just expect him to accept it. Call a solicitor, arrange a DNA test and apologise to your bloody son."

Handing her the business card I turn and walk away from her. She shouts some sort of obscenity at me, but I ignore it, more due to the fact that my head is about to explode. I am shaking and about to burst into tears, but I make it out of the park and find Steven talking angrily into his phone. Gerry, who had obviously been summoned while I was dealing with Leah, pulls up next to the kerb in the Range Rover. Steven continues his conversation while I get Georgie into the car. Gerry folds the pram with minimal effort and as soon as I have the car seat strapped in and I am safely in the car with the door shut, I let go. The tears run down my face and drip onto my scarf. I look at Georgie who is still sound asleep and has been the whole time. I put my hands in my hair and squeeze them into fists. I literally want to rip my hair out. I'm so pissed off. This is yet another set-back. When the hell are we going to catch a break?

Steven gets into the front passenger seat, still on the phone.

"I don't know if she's telling the truth, the last time I saw her was about seven or eight years ago. We weren't even together that long."

I can hear a muffled voice coming from the other end of the line, but I can't make out what they are saying.

"State the fucking obvious Lucas. I don't need a lecture on how babies are made. Okay, I'll come in and see you on Monday and we can discuss how to make this shit disappear. Yes thanks, bye." He hangs up and rubs his forehead. "Fuck," he shouts making Georgie stir slightly.

Make it disappear? After me telling Leah that he would step up to the plate, he just wants to make it disappear. What if the kid really is his? Isn't he man enough to take on the responsibility? The thought of it hits me like a punch to the gut. This is not a side to Steven I ever thought I'd see, and I don't know that I like it.

"Who is Lucas?" I ask as Gerry pulls away from the kerb.

Steven ignores me but I notice Gerry give him a look that speaks volumes. He sighs. "He's my lawyer."

He sounds almost defeated and stares straight out of the window ahead. I want to ask him so many questions, but I fear it will make things worse, so I simply nod and stay silent the rest of the short ride home.

CHAPTER 13

I WAKE TO THE sound of a piano playing. Steven spent the rest of the afternoon and evening in his office so Georgie and I watched TV until it was bedtime. I honestly don't even know if he came to bed. I know I need to let him deal with this horrible situation, but I also want him to know that I am here for him. I know he is hurting and I can imagine a bombshell like that is enough to freak anyone out, especially someone who has been through as much as Steven has. Making my way downstairs I hear him singing a lullaby. The sight that greets me as I look over the bannister melts my heart. Steven is sitting at the piano and Georgie is resting on his bare upper body. He has one hand supporting her and is using the other to play. He looks so natural with her like that and I feel my eyes start to fill. He stops playing and smiles when he realises I am there.

"We didn't want to disturb you," Steven whispers and Georgie stirs slightly.

"You're a natural. She must be missing her mummy and daddy."

Joining him at the piano, I give Georgie's little hand a rub.

"How do you feel having her here Gina? I mean after finding out you weren't pregnant."

His question throws me. I love having her here, but I understand why he is asking. I was really gutted when the test was negative, and I get the feeling that the more time he has to process everything the more he feels the same way I did.

"I'm fine. I know I was disappointed but I'm past the point of letting the things that happen to me affect how I live. I'm damn sure not going to let it stop me enjoying this little bundle."

"That's my girl," he says. "I think this wee one is out for the count. I'm pretty sure I can feel drool on my shoulder."

I laugh quietly as he stands. "She's not the only female who drools over you," I say with a smile.

Steven shakes his head and rolls his eyes at me and I watch as he climbs the stairs to take Georgie back to her little travel cot in our bedroom. My heart is full to bursting with love for him. He has so much light in his soul and I count myself very lucky that I get to see it.

Sitting down at the piano I clink on a few keys. I would love to be able to play like Steven does. I could watch him play for hours. I head for the kitchen to get a warm drink. I'm shivering even though the house is warm. The clock on the oven reads 1.45. Brilliant, I'm wide awake. I think a hot chocolate will do the trick. As I set about heating the milk and filling two mugs with chocolate powder, Steven appears in the doorway.

"Baby is down and still sound asleep."

"Good. Steven, we need to talk about what happened today."

I know this is going to be hard, but we need to sort it out. He nods and takes a seat at the breakfast bar while I finish making the hot chocolates. Placing a mug down in front of Steven I take a seat next to him.

"I'm so sorry Gina. We are being seriously tested aren't we?" Steven sighs.

"You don't say," I smile in agreement.

He takes my hand. "Gina, I spoke out of turn today. No, I spoke out of anger when I was talking to Lucas. I never expected to see Leah again never mind her turning up with a kid and claiming he's mine."

"Do you think he could be yours?"

"I hate to say it, but it's possible. He looked about seven or so and that's how long it's been since I last saw Leah. After she emailed me to tell me she had left

113

I never heard from her again. I don't even know if she actually went to the States or not."

"Well I told her to talk to a solicitor and organize a DNA test. The reason I wanted to give her your business card was so that she didn't have your personal details. This needs to be done properly, more for the sake of that poor wee boy than anything else. Did you see his face when she was going off on one?"

Steven smiles at me. "You know Gina if you weren't with me when I saw her, I don't think this would be settled in any sort of amicable way. She's just as much of a bitch as she's always been." He leans in and kisses my lips lightly. "You're my saving grace."

I shake my head.

"I only did what I thought was right. Do you think it was a coincidence she was in the park today? The more I've thought about it the more I think she was there with the purpose of bumping in to you. It's not hard to find out where you work."

"I thought the same thing. If she had taken her kid to the park regularly I would have seen her before now. I'm pissed at how she went about this, but I'm not surprised. Remember I told you she always had to be the centre of attention? This isn't about her son knowing his dad, it's about her staking a claim."

"She thought Georgie was ours."

Steven smiles. "Really?"

"Yeah, she said my kid better get used to not having a daddy when you fuck off and leave me."

He takes a drink from his mug. "She really is a piece of work. I don't even know why I ever wanted to be with her."

"Let's just get on with our lives and deal with whatever happens when it happens."

"Sounds good to me. Fancy taking these in to watch TV? I'm wide awake and you look like you are too."

"Absolutely handsome, lead the way."

I jump down from my stool and grab my mug. Steven takes my other hand and lifts it up to his lips.

"I love you Gina," he whispers against my knuckles as we make our way out of the kitchen.

***

Spring sunlight streams in through the open blinds and casts strips of yellow light across the bed. Steven is reading the Sunday papers and I am sorting out the new-born photos I took of Georgie, who is asleep in her little cot. I can hear her tiny breaths and when she makes a little noise, we both look at each other and smile.

Someday. The thought pops into my mind and it gives me butterflies. It's obvious I can see myself with this man for the rest of my life. I wonder for a moment if he feels the same. I wonder if we can live happily ever after or if there will always be something to thwart any attempt at a normal life.

When I was younger I always thought I would be a mum in my twenties and have a great career and a wonderful husband. I never imagined I'd be a widow in my thirties and that my marriage wasn't all it seemed. If our lives were picture perfect we'd be a pretty boring species.

Georgie lets out a loud cry and Steven goes to her cot and lifts her into his arms.

"Hey little darling, you hungry?" He whispers to her as he brings her to the bed and places her in the middle.

"I'll get her some milk. Would you like a coffee?"

"Yes please," he says as I make my way down to the kitchen.

Listening to the coffee machine making whirring and gurgling noises, my mind drifts, thinking and rethinking the events in the park yesterday. I have run endless scenarios through my mind over the last twenty hours. What if the little boy is Steven's? Could I fit someone else's child into my life right now? It's taking me all my time to get to grips with this new relationship without adding more people to the mix. I also can't help but feel sorry for that child. It's bad enough that he doesn't know who his dad is but for his mother to try and out Steven in front of him is despicable. My little internal quandary is disturbed by Steven's arrival at the kitchen door.

"What you thinking?" He asks as Georgie snoozes in his arms.

"Eh?"

"Your eyebrows are about to kiss each other."

I relax the muscles I didn't even know I was using. This is something I've always suffered from. My facial expressions and body language give me away every time. I can have no secrets.

"Oh nothing."

"Liar," he says, a knowing smile curling at his lips.

I shake my head in defeat. "I've had a lot of time over the last few weeks to think about my life and where it's going. More so after... well you know."

I hate to even mention the abduction to Steven. It's one of those subjects that I know we need to talk about, but I just feel that it's too raw for both of us. I've managed to keep it out of my mind as much as I can. Nate has helped me a lot, but I don't really know how Steven feels about it. Sure the counselling helps but we haven't actually sat down and talked on our own. I know I will break down and I don't want to put any more pressure on Steven, especially not now.

"Okay so where do you think it's going?"

"I see you in it. Of course I see you in it. I love you Steven you know that."

He sits at the table and stares out the window. As he does, Georgie stirs and wakes.

"I know that Gina, more so now after what happened yesterday. I don't know why you haven't run for the hills yet."

"Why on earth would I?"

I hand him the warmed bottle and sit across from him, watching as he effortlessly feeds Georgie as though he's done it a million times. He shakes his head and gives a tiny smile. "You're an amazing woman, don't ever change."

It's a slight change of subject but I don't care. I've said all I need to, he knows I'm here, and I'm not going anywhere.

CHAPTER 14

"SO, I CAN AUTHORISE the six hundred K as soon as the charity is registered?"

I'm sitting on the sofa in Steven's home office watching him talking on the phone with his accountant. Georgie went home this morning and we have spent the last four hours working on a plan for setting up a foundation to help kids in the care system get the best out of their lives once they are on their own. It has been an eye opening morning in many respects. I have had a real insight into how hard it can be for people in care to cope when they have to go out on their own. Not every young adult is as strong willed as Steven was or has as much to prove as he thought he did.

I've also learned a lot about how Steven coped when he left the care system. He was given an opportunity, through his high school, to attend summer school courses at Glasgow University and that set him on the right path. He says, had it not been for that he might never have ended up where he is now. The big problem with that type of scheme is that it is limited to certain schools, from the most deprived areas, so not everyone gets the opportunity to participate. It's a shame but it all boils down to money.

Our initial plan at this stage is to allow those kids in care who are in their last two years at high school, where summer school opportunities are not offered for free, to apply for a grant to pay for the course. It's a starting point and we know not everyone wants to go to university or is academically able to but if we can make enough through charitable donations in the first few years, we can expand to include apprenticeships in the future.

Watching Steven today, seeing how enthusiastic he is makes me love him even more. He is so passionate about changing young people's lives for the better and ultimately contributing to a better society. Okay, so we know we are not going to change the world and there will always be some that can't be helped but if we can make a difference to even one young person it is better than none at all.

Steven hangs up the phone and leans back in his chair. His smile is infectious, and I smile back.

"Good news then?"

"Oh yes. I can release the funds as soon as we get the charity registered and Donald will take care of everything else. Working next door to your accountant has its perks."

"That's fab news. I'll get the applications sorted and, in the meantime, we need a name."

Steven shrugs his shoulders. "I hadn't thought about that you know. I kind of got swept up in the moment. I would say the name should reflect the purpose, but we need it to be flexible so that it can accommodate expansion."

"Ooh you've got your wee business head on now haven't you?"

"You better believe it my dear. I really want to make this a success and my God do I have a million ideas floating around my head already."

He's so animated I can't help but smile.

"Slow down soldier we've only just started talking about this, my brain is going to give up soon."

He puts his hands behind his head and rests his legs on the desk. "Right a name, let's get cracking."

An hour later, and Steven and I are standing in the kitchen with an A4 piece of paper in front of us. We're on our fourth coffee today and I feel as high as a kite.

"I don't think any of these names fit you know," I scrunch up my nose.

"Hmm, you're right," Steven says hugging his mug

to his chest. "I think we're missing something. These names just don't represent what the vision of the charity is."

I smile at the spark in his eyes. It's as though this project has ignited something in him. Maybe it's because this is an opportunity to pay forward the help he was given as a teenager. I dread to think what could have become of him if no-one had helped him. I had a privileged life growing up and getting to know the struggle Steven had has made me realise that many skilled people get lost in the system because of a lack of opportunities.

"I have it."

"Whoa woman I nearly spilled my coffee," says a startled Steven.

"Opportunities for Life."

Steven smiles and nods. "It's perfect. You're perfect."

He kisses my nose and I can't help smiling.

I score through all the names on the list and write our new name in big capital letters.

OPPORTUNITIES FOR LIFE

It looks absolutely amazing. It's so simple but that's the beauty of it.

The ringing of Steven's phone cut's through the

happy atmosphere. A shiver runs down my spine when I see the expression on Steven's face. It has turned dark and angry and I fear our upbeat morning is about to turn sour.

"It's Lucas. I have to take this," he says walking into the living room.

I stay in the kitchen, but I can hear every word through the open door. I wonder to myself if that was intentional. I have already told him that he needs to stop shutting me out so maybe this is his way of trying. I listen as he talks to Lucas.

"What the fuck? Are you serious or am I being pranked? Jeremy Kyle? This has got to be a joke."

I'm rooted to the spot, straining to hear every word.

"Sorry mate, I'm.. huh I just don't know what to say. You know I'm not going to do this right?"

I'm getting the gist of the one sided conversation.

"Ok, I'll come in tomorrow morning and we'll sort this out. Thanks Lucas."

I venture into the living room and Steven turns to me with a perplexed look on his face.

"You ok?"

"Did you hear that? I swear to God Gina she's gone too far."

"I assume by '*she*' you mean Leah. What does she want?" Even as I ask the question, I know what the answer will be.

"She wants me to take a DNA test for her kid. That's fair enough. I'm more than willing to do it Gina. It's obviously not enough to do it privately though, she wants to go on fucking TV and do it. I can't do it. It's so degrading."

I can't help myself but laugh. It's like laughing at a funeral. I know it's inappropriate, but I can't stop.

"How can she think this is good for her son? I feel so sorry for that poor little guy. The way she acted in the park was bad enough but to do this in front of millions of people, it's downright disgusting behaviour for a parent," I say.

"I know and I'll tell you something else, if that boy *is* my son, I'm going to seek custody, she's not a fit mother."

I feel as though I've been punched in the gut. There's no more room for laughter.

"Are you sure that's a good idea? Yes, it's shocking to do this to the wee boy but you can't force a child who doesn't know you to leave his mother. Sure, get access and visitation but please don't do anything out of spite."

"Spite? Gina she is the one who started this not me. If I had known about the boy I would have been there from the start, you of all people should know that. There's no way I would ever want any child to never know both its parents and be loved by them."

124

I don't know what to do. This whole situation is becoming a bit surreal. I put my hand on Steven's and rub his knuckles. He closes his eyes and shakes his head.

"I'm sorry," his voice is solemn and soaked in guilt.

"This isn't your fault Steven, don't you dare apologise for any of this. I'm here and I'm not going anywhere. We'll get through this, I promise."

He pulls me in to his arms and rests his chin on my head. I feel some of the tension in his body go as he lets out a long sigh.

"You don't need this stress right now Gina, not with the exhibition opening tomorrow so we'll let Lucas take care of everything. There has to be a way to get her to drop this stupid notion of going on a bloody TV show."

I move so that I can look up at him. This is all so unfair. It would be lovely to catch a break at some point. I feel like every time we make a little headway in our relationship something comes along to upend it.

"Let's go for lunch and a drink. I don't know about you, but my nerves are all over the place."

Steven nods and smiles but doesn't let me go. I'm fine with that. When we are together like this it's easier to shut out the world.

CHAPTER 15

MY DAD IS ONE of those people that is very 'go with the flow'. He has been, for my entire existence, a very honest man who enjoys simple pleasures and is happy with his lot in life. It had never occurred to me that he could in any way be flawed. Heroes aren't allowed to have flaws and more often than not a girl's dad is her hero. The day I saw my dad with another woman was the day he fell off the huge pedestal I had built for him. I know she is a woman he used to work with but watching the very personal interaction between them made me sick to my stomach. Ever since that day, any time I have seen my dad, I have wanted so badly to confront him, but I think in the back of my mind I have been scared of what it may reveal.

Having had a weekend full of revelations and horrible surprises, I have decided in my infinite wisdom that one more would be a good idea. Either that or it will be just enough to push me over the edge. So here I sit, at a table in the back of a little artisan café on Byres Road, waiting patiently for my dad to come and meet me.

"Can I get you anything else?" asks the young blonde waitress as she clears my coffee cup from the table.

"I'm good for the moment. I'm meeting someone here shortly, so we'll order when he gets here."

"No problem," she smiles.

I move to pull my phone from my pocket and my breath catches as I see my dad at the door. I try to compose myself, but I have already got myself so wound up about what is to come that it's almost impossible.

"Hello my darling," he says as he nears the table. "This was a lovely surprise to get to see you today. We don't do this often enough."

I stand and greet him with a hug and a kiss and all at once wish I could just let this go. "Hey daddy."

He takes the seat across from me and busies himself with taking off his jacket and grabbing a menu to look at.

"I've never been in here before it's very nice. What do you recommend?" He smiles as he looks up from the menu.

The look on his face confirms what I have just realised. The build-up of different emotion of the last few days coupled with the unknown of how this conversation is going to go has boiled over and now I am a snivelling wreck.

"Oh, Gina darling what's wrong?" My dad gets up and sits on the seat beside me, pulling me in to his arms and stroking my hair the same way he always has whenever I have been this upset. That simply makes the situation worse.

"Who is Andrea Marshall?" I blurt out through my tears. This is not how I imagined the conversation going but it's out there now so there's no going back.

"She's an ex colleague but why do you ask?" He says as he lets me go and sits back a little so that he can see me.

"I saw you both together in the park and I'm sorry dad, but she looked like more than just an ex colleague." I wipe the tears from my eyes with the napkin from my coffee earlier.

My dad narrows his eyes suspiciously at me and is about to speak when the same blonde waitress comes to the table.

"Hi folks can I get you anything?" I can tell she has witnessed my little meltdown and her question seems to be aimed at more than cake and coffee.

"I would say a couple of hot chocolates with all the

trimmings is in order wouldn't you Gina?"

"Mhm." It's all I can muster and as the waitress leaves the table my dad gets up and takes his original seat so that he is facing me again.

"Well where do I start?" He says as he leans forward and clasps his hands on the table.

"Why don't you tell me what was going on that day? Dad I love you with all my heart, but I swear if you've been cheating on mum I'll…"

"Jesus Gina how on earth can you think that? I'm so sorry you've got that impression. I love your mother to the ends of the earth and I'd never do that to her or you."

I feel like a horrible person now as I see the hurt in his eyes.

"Let me explain sweetheart and I'm sure you'll understand."

We are quiet a moment as the waitress puts the most delicious looking hot chocolates down on the table. Dad spoons a melting marshmallow into his moth before he speaks, and I ready myself for his explanation.

"Andrea and I worked together for over twenty years. Mum and I have been friendly with her and her husband Tony for almost as long. You met her a few times when you were younger, but you probably wouldn't really have remembered her. Anyway, Tony passed away at the end of May last year. We hadn't seen them for a couple of years since Andrea retired a year before me. We didn't even know he had been ill." He stops to take a drink and continues. "So Andrea called a few weeks ago and told mum all about Tony and asked for our help. She and Tony had lived in a huge house and it became too much for her on her own. She had made a decision to sell everything and move to Australia to be with her daughter and three grandkids."

"God dad I'm really sad to hear that. It's a shame you didn't know at the time."

"It really is but Andrea had heard about Aiden and didn't think it was appropriate to burden us with her troubles." My heart sinks as I realise that, again, Aiden's death didn't only affect me.

"Oh, I'm so sorry."

"Gina honey we don't blame you. You are the most important person in our lives and you, and your wellbeing is all that matters to us. I honestly think she was right. News like that may have been too much for us to handle so soon. I assume you saw us at the fountain yes?"

"Yes, I did. I was on my way to the gallery to meet with Ellen."

"In that case you had only missed your mother by about ten minutes. We had actually just come from the art gallery tearoom. I put Andrea in touch with Steven. I knew he would be able to help her. He has a lot of contacts and she needed to get a good return for her house to fund her move. I've since heard that she managed to sell it really quickly so he must have done something right."

I sit back and sigh as, yet again, I feel like a prize idiot. I'm positively disgusted with myself for even thinking that my dad was a cheat and even more so for the horrible things that have gone through my mind in the days since I saw them together.

"Dad I'm so sorry for accusing you like that. I have some serious issues I still need to work on. My trust has gone right out the window since I found out about Aiden."

"Sweetheart you've been through so much in this short while, but I'll tell you something for nothing, mum and I couldn't be prouder of you. You're like the Terminator, you keep bouncing back."

"Well I've been likened to a lot of things but that's a new one," I laugh as I take his big, warm hand. "In all seriousness though dad I am sorry not just for this but for everything you and mum have had to deal with. You guys should be enjoying your retirement not worrying about me."

"Honey you'll realise when you have your own children that you never stop worrying about them."

His words about children reminds me of the Leah situation and I suppose now is as good a time as any to tell him about it.

"On that note, lets order some lunch. I have something to tell you and I'm afraid it might take a while."

He shakes his head, smiles and lifts the menu.

"One of everything then?" He laughs.

CHAPTER 16

THE CHAMPAGNE FLUTE I was handed when I came in to the Art Gallery is beaded with condensation and I haven't touched a drop. My hands are a little shaky and I feel as though I am going to be sick. There are no members of the public here yet only friends and family of the artists, invited guests and the artists themselves. My photos have been blown up onto massive canvases and, even if I do say so myself, they look amazing. Steven is chatting with my parents and Charlie and Mark are on their way. I take the quiet time to have a look at the other artist's photos.

The first set is by a woman named Sylvia. I met her when I arrived here this evening. I reckon she is in her seventies and looks very elegant, kind of like Helen Mirren. Her photos are black and white and depict elderly people. She travelled to India last year and took the photos at a church. The contrast in them is striking, the mix of light and dark picking out the wrinkles on their faces and the wisdom in their eyes. My mum keeps trying to catch my eye, her face beaming with pride so much that I feel a little embarrassed. I turn away from her gaze because I know if I don't I will burst into tears. I give my attention to some of the other photos and before long I am mesmerised. Artists have a completely unique way of approaching their subject. It becomes almost like a signature. I know when I take pictures I like to play around with the fore and backgrounds. These can be more interesting than the subject itself. Sometimes you can catch something unexpected and fascinating. Although, I have had the odd occasion where I have managed to catch something no gallery owner would ever want to see. Let's just say one of those involved a dog and the call of nature during a woodland photo shoot for some kids. I always keep all of my photos, but this was one that went straight into the recycle bin.

I feel Steven's heat and presence before I even turn around. My face fills with a huge smile as he slips his arms round my waist. He leans in and whispers, "You're the talk of the town tonight."

I turn in his arms. "Really?"

"Oh yes. See that man in the pinstripe suit?" He points to a tall fellow with dark hair and the most fantastic tan I have ever seen in February in Glasgow.

I nod.

"He's from Highland Hideaways and he really likes your Aurora pictures. They promote the Highlands and Islands all over the world. I heard him talking to Ellen about them. Want to know what he said, or would you prefer I let Ellen tell you?"

"Oh my God, you are so cruel, you know I hate surprises." I squeal and hit him on the arm.

"You don't have to beat it out of me I'll tell you. Do you really want to know?"

"Steven, I swear I am on the edge tonight as it is, stop teasing me."

"I don't know, I think I am having too much fun right now."

"That's it! I'm going to ask Ellen myself." As I try to escape from his arms his grip tightens.

"Okay, I'm sorry, I'll stop. He asked Ellen to introduce him to the artist with a view to commissioning a new set of photos for the Highland Hideaways website."

All at once a nauseous feeling creeps its way up from my toes. Without a word to Steven I shake his grip and run to try and find the closest toilet. The champagne flute gives up most of its contents as it sloshes all over the floor. The art gallery is so vast that I am lost in no time and before I know it, I'm too late.

The only thing I can find to puke in is a little waste paper bin and so, in such an unladylike fashion, I find myself on my knees with my head in a bucket. If Mr Pinstripe-tourist-man sees this awful display he'll be running for the door.

"Gina are you okay?"

The sound of Steven's voice adds to my shame. I shake my head.

"Oh God Steven I've just made a rip-roaring arse of myself, haven't I?"

I take the paper napkin he hands me, but I can't bear to look at him.

"Hey." He gets down on his knees beside me and pulls my chin with his finger so that I am forced to look at him. "I shouldn't have told you like that, I'm sorry. I was so excited for you and I love to see your face light up."

"It was such a shock, but I really haven't felt right all day. My nerves are shot."

He shakes his head and smiles.

"Come with me." Steven stands and holds out his hand to me.

We don't go back in the direction of the exhibition but instead climb the stairs to the first floor.

"Where are we going? People will be arriving soon, and I don't think we are supposed to be up here after hours."

"Since when do we follow convention and rules Gina?"

The heat in his smile tells me all I need to know. The gallery is dimly lit at this late hour casting shadows and hiding places in every nook and cranny. And it's into one of those nooks that I now find myself pushed hard against the wall. As Steven kisses me, I am about to protest that I have, in fact, just been sick and my mouth is not exactly the most hospitable environment when he pushes a half consumed oval mint past my lips.

"Do you feel ok?"

"Yes," I manage a whisper.

"Good."

He smiles as he places light kisses on my neck, moving ever so slowly down to skim the tops of my breasts with his glorious lips. The light touch of his finger circling my nipple over my dress sends shivers down my entire body and knowing where we are makes this all the more exciting. I'm taken by surprise when Steven lifts the front of my dress and slips his hand into my knickers. My gasp is twinned with his as he finds me already wet.

"Woman you're fucking killing me."

I can't help but snigger. "Come on you know I can't help my wanton body when it comes to you."

He leans his forehead on mine and closes his eyes.

"We should get back. As much as I don't want to, your guests will be getting suspicious."

Steven lets me go and abruptly moves away leaving me feeling bereft. I hate how needy my body is around him.

We make our way back to the exhibition. The place is now filled with people admiring the works or chatting about them. I stop at the door and take in the scene. I could never have imagined in this short space of time that I would be showing my work in an art gallery, let alone this spectacularly beautiful one.

"Gina, I have been looking everywhere for you." Ellen heads towards me with a huge smile on her face. As she reaches me, she grabs both of my arms.

"I have the best news for you. Oh I am so proud."

"I'll leave you both to it. I'm going to find your dad."

Steven kisses my cheek and smiles at Ellen, who gives him a wink. I feel like I am on the outside of an inside secret.

"Gina, this is going to blow you away." Ellen says turning her full attention back to me. "Highland Hideaways want to use your pictures in their new advertising campaign. I can't tell you how proud I am of you."

"Sorry if I look like I'm not enjoying this more but Steven kind of already let it slip to me and I have already puked my canapés up over it."

"Oh honey I'm sorry." Ellen rubs my arm. "You really don't give yourself the credit you deserve you know Gina."

"Thank you Ellen. Do people like that normally turn up randomly at these events? I thought this evening was invite only?"

"It is. His office called and asked for the invite." She wrinkles her nose. "I didn't think there was anything strange about it. Given the amount of local gallery showings there are all over Scotland at any one time, I don't really know why he chose ours."

"I bet I do." I look in the direction of where Steven is chatting with my dad.

"Oh Gina, do you think Steven put in a good word for you. That's so romantic."

"Or a little bit over presumptuous."

Ellen's eyebrows knit together. "Can I give you a little bit of advice honey? Don't ever turn down any help you can get. So, your man knows people in high places, word of mouth is the best advertising you can get. I'll tell you, if that man hadn't been here tonight, I would have had you submit your work to a company like his anyway."

"Thank you Ellen, your belief in me is more than I could ask for."

"Honey, I know talent when I see it. I've been in

this game a long time you know. Simon absolutely adores your work too. And we're not the only ones."

I smile at her, remembering meeting them both at the art gallery. I could tell there was more to their relationship than work. I follow her gaze as she mentions his name and see that she is watching him as intently as I sometimes catch myself watching Steven

"You two are such a lovely couple, thank you for taking me under your wing."

"Oh honey, *we* only show the work, you're the artist. Now let's go and meet this man and get you both acquainted."

CHAPTER 17

GERRY HOLDS MY DOOR open as Steven holds my hand to steady me. I haven't even had that much to drink but my head is fuzzy; I know it has more to do with the excitement of my encounter with a certain Mr Johnson from Highland Hideaways. In the same night as I was part of an exhibition showing my work, I now have a contract to loom over, with a view to loaning my work. Not only that, but my photos will become the backdrop to the new campaign for boosting their tourism in Scotland.

"What did you do Mr Parker?" I ask giving Steven a sly look.

"What do you mean?"

"I think you know what I mean," I say pointing a finger at him.

"I think you've had too much to drink. I have no

idea what you are talking about."

"Don't play dumb with me, I know you contacted the Highland Hideaways office and got them to be there. I'm not daft you know."

As I playfully try to poke his shoulder, he grabs my wrist and pins it behind my back, then does the same with the other. The moment he reaches for his tie, the atmosphere changes. As I look into his eyes, desire burns through me and I know that the prelude to this moment has kept us both hot and wanting all night. The art gallery was never going to be an appropriate place for us tonight but here, in our own space, we can be as free as we want.

Steven pulls his now loosened tie teasingly slowly through the collar of his shirt and sets about tying my hands together behind my back. It's not tight and I know I could easily free myself. I won't though. I have taken rather a liking to being tied up. It was never something I had thought of before; my last relationship was as simple as you could get. It's a wonder we didn't have a schedule.

Steven runs his finger down my cheek and lets it linger on my lips. "You amaze me every day. Every minute of every day," he whispers as he lowers his lips to mine.

The kiss is hard and passionate, and I am desperate to put my hands up and touch his face.

"Turn around," he says in a low voice.

As I do, he leads me to the foot of the stairs.

"Go upstairs, sit on the bed and wait for me. Do not touch the tie."

I make my way up the stairs as Steven disappears into the living room and out of sight. I'm all at once intrigued and hesitant. I have no idea what he has planned but the heat in his eyes spoke volumes. I'm also a little worried that I may lose my balance and fall down the stairs.

As I sit on the bed with my back to the door, the anticipation of what is to come has my body shivering. Steven has a way of making me always want more. I close my eyes just as the loveliest piano music starts to play in the room. It's all at once intense and soothing.

"Keep your eyes closed," I hear Steven say over the music.

I do as I'm told and my breath catches in my throat when I feel him touch my cheek. He cups my chin and kisses me, oh, so gently. I let out a little moan as his lips leave mine. I feel him lean over me and he undoes the tie on my wrists.

"Stand up."

I open my eyes. Steven is standing in front of me dressed only in the black suit trousers that he was wearing at the gallery. The sight almost buckles my knees. His body is toned and beautiful, he could easily be one of those renaissance sculptures. I lick my lips at the sight of him.

"You have a choice here tonight," he starts to undress me as he talks. "Soft or hard?" He whispers as he lets my dress pool at my feet. "Fast or slow?" He unclips my bra and slowly pulls it over my arms.

My entire body is on fire as I stand almost naked before him. Steven gets down on his knees in front of me and hooks his fingers over the top of my knickers. He looks up at me with more composure than I have at this moment.

"Your choice," he says as he starts to slide my underwear down my legs at a teasingly slow pace.

"Hard and slow," my voice is raspy and goose bumps have formed over my skin.

"Hmm… good choice."

I step out of my knickers and dress and Steven stands up. He places his thumb on my lips and painfully slowly runs it down the entire length of my torso. He stops as he reaches just below my navel. With the same slow, controlled movement he slides his thumb from one hipbone to the other, deliberately skimming my sex with his fingers. I close my eyes and breathe in deeply, my body shuddering under the tension building in me.

He drags each of his hands up either side of my body and then down my back. Cupping my bum cheeks, he pulls me in to him. He is as hard as stone and I can't help my body trying to writhe against him.

"Uh uh, not yet, this is the slow you asked for," he says inching back from me. He is hardly touching me and yet my body is about to explode.

"Is that the hard?" I whisper gesturing to his crotch.

"Naughty girl Gina," Steven says putting his hand in his pocket and pulling out a length of the same black rope he used to tie me up in my apartment. This one is a lot longer.

"Hmm, what are you intending to do with that?"

"Lie down. From now on you don't get to touch me."

This is going to take some serious willpower. I lie in the middle of the bed and Steven straddles me. He pulls my hands down and ties them both together at the wrists. It seems I won't really have a choice as to whether or not I get to touch him. Taking the ends of the rope he leans up over me to tie them to the hooks holding the swag of fabric at the head of the bed. His lithe body is so close to my mouth that I can't help myself but lick him. His muscles ripple as he gives a little laugh. When he has finished tying the ropes he leans in close to my ear. His breath hot and slow.

"I'm going to make you pay for that."

I gasp at the tone of his voice. It's dominating and sexy as hell. Steven moves to the end of the bed and I raise my head slightly to see what he is doing. He pulls me down gently until the rope holding my wrists is taught. He has two more pieces of rope in his hands and proceeds to tie them round my ankles and secure them to the foot of the bed so that my legs are spread wide. I am completely at his mercy and I feel a little vulnerable. The tightness of the ropes limits my movements and I am slightly apprehensive about what he has planned. Right at this moment I am rather regretting touching him.

When I am fully bound, Steven tests the ropes and nods to himself. He stands up at the foot of the bed and puts his hands in his pockets. He looks at his handy work with pride and I feel a little embarrassed. I close my eyes against the redness creeping over my body. When I feel his cool hands on my shins a shiver runs through my entire being, goose bumps appearing everywhere and my nipples becoming painfully hard.

"Keep your eyes closed, it'll heighten your other senses."

He moves his hands slowly up my legs and I am willing him to touch me where I need it most. But he doesn't. Instead he moves his hands up my torso, between my breasts and down my arms. He has literally missed every erogenous zone on my body, yet my skin is on fire. There is a hot, electrified trail where his hands have been. I want so badly to press my legs together to ease the pressure. The tension building in me is torturous and I know he sees it.

His hands are gone but I am aware of him near me. I want so much to open my eyes, to see his beautiful face and body. To see how he looks at me, how much his eyes adore me. But I don't, because Steven was right. Keeping my eyes closed has made even the smallest touch seem intense. I startle slightly when the foot of the bed dips between my legs. I feel Steven's heat near my skin and his hot breath on my sex. When I feel his tongue on me, I am all but done for. He obviously senses that too and takes me as close to coming as he can then stops and moves abruptly off the bed.

"Oh God," I moan and try to writhe on the bed to get some relief, obviously in vain since I am so well trussed up.

"Taste yourself Gina," Steven's voice is low and he kisses me hard, forcing his tongue into my mouth. He puts his cool fingers between my legs and strokes me ever so softly. I will him to do it harder, to stop teasing me and give me the release I need. As soon as he knows I am almost there he stops again, and I can do nothing but beg.

"Please Steven," my voice is a whimper.

"Hard and slow you asked for Gina. The hard part is dealing with this delayed gratification. I'll get you there, slowly."

Oh my God how long is he planning to keep this up? I wonder if anyone has ever died from this type of torture. Movement at the foot of the bed interrupts my thoughts. I feel him loom over me then he is stroking me again but not with his hand. I can't stop my body from reacting to his touch. I squeeze my eyes shut as the tension builds again. He stops for a few seconds, just enough time for me to calm slightly, then he starts again. He does this over and over until I am almost seeing stars; I honestly think I may pass out.

"I think you're ready now," Steven whispers, placing his hands on either side of my head.

"That's a fucking understatement," my voice is breathy and full of want and my arms are starting to tire from being tied for so long. Steven pushes himself inside me ever so slowly. It seems he's not finished with the slow quite yet. I don't care; the feeling of him filling me is exquisite.

Now the slow ceases and the hard begins again. I think this delayed gratification has got the better of Steven too. He thrusts hard into me and my body bucks as much as it can. With one hand still on the bed he quickly unties my wrists and rubs them hard, bringing feeling back to them.

"Open your eyes."

I do as I'm told, and the dim light lets me look

directly at him without being blinded. Steven puts his hands under me and sits us both up. At last I can touch him and it's fantastic. It's like dieting, the more you're denied something the better it is when you get it. He reaches behind him and unties my ankles, rubbing each of them. His hands are behind my back again and he starts to move his hips against me, hitting a sweet delicious spot deep inside me. I move my legs so that I am straddling Steven's lap and finally take what I have been craving since the museum, which seems a million hours ago now.

As I move faster and faster, a wondrous heat spreads over my entire body and I come in waves around him, my muscles quivering all over as I expel all of the evenings pent up tension. Steven pushes me onto the bed and pulls out of me. Quickly discarding his condom, he leans over me and proceeds to finish himself off. It's so goddamn hot that I can't help but touch myself. I'm totally mesmerised by this uninhibited display that I come again and so does he, spilling himself over my belly. We stay still for a moment staring into each other's eyes. We are connected, physically and mentally and I am a little overwhelmed at the feelings this man evokes in me.

"I love you Gina," he kisses me so softly and tenderly that it makes me want to cry.

CHAPTER 18

OOH THAT HURTS. I stretch out in bed as I open my eyes to the beautiful morning light. Catching a glimpse of my wrist I see a slight red mark. I look at the other and it's the same. The sight should horrify me but instead I smile, remembering the intense feelings of being tied up and helpless. I honestly never thought I'd be into that sort of kinky stuff, but it excites me. It's as though Steven has awakened subconscious fantasies in me that no one else ever could.

I feel my body ache all over as I turn to snuggle into Steven, but I find his side of the bed empty. Grabbing my phone to check the time, I see it is almost 10am. Last night really did take it out of me. Pulling a robe off the hook behind the door I make my way out of the bedroom. I catch my reflection in the full-length mirror on the landing and it makes me stop.

My hair still has the curls I got put in yesterday and my eye makeup is slightly smudged giving me a sexy sultry look. I have the robe held against my body and look at the curve of my hips and the shape of my legs. I feel as though I am looking at myself through new eyes, through Steven's eyes. I never used to feel pretty or beautiful, but the way Steven lavishes his attention on me and tells me I am every day has given me renewed body confidence. I smile and head downstairs letting the robe slip to the floor on the small middle landing.

I tiptoe downstairs and hear Steven talking. Even better, he's on the phone so I can sneak up on him. I walk through the lounge and see his back. He's leaning on the breakfast bar. I walk through the double doors. Steven is not alone. A man sits at the table with a mug in his hand and his mouth agape as he appraises my nakedness.

I about turn and run to the downstairs bathroom. I am utterly mortified. I have no idea who that man is or what he is doing here. Pulling a towel around my now not so-confident-body I look in the mirror. *Yeah, not so sexy now you twit.* There's a knock at the door.

"Gina can I come in?"

"I suppose so," I can hear the defeat in my voice.

He opens the door and smiles. "Well that was an entrance and a half."

151

I smack his arm. "Please don't make fun of me Steven, I'm so embarrassed."

"I'm sorry. Come here."

I reluctantly let him pull me into a hug. He puts his chin on the top of my head.

"Who is that anyway?"

"Lucas, my lawyer."

I bury my head into his chest. "Oh no Steven, I'm so sorry."

"Hey, don't you apologise." He leans back to look at me. "Lucas didn't see much."

"That's not the point, and not true. He saw everything. Every time I try to be confident and sexy, I always make a fool of myself."

Steven shakes his head. "Gina, you're the most confident, sexy woman I have ever known. Will you please stop putting yourself down? I swear if Lucas wasn't here, I'd have fucked you on the bloody kitchen floor." He leans in and kisses me softly. "Now go and throw some clothes on and come and meet Lucas properly. You'll like him."

"Yeah okay, I'll go and put on the biggest jumper I can find." I try for a sarcastic smile but I'm dying inside.

***

Steven and Lucas stop talking as I walk into the

kitchen. Lucas stands and holds out his hand to me. He has a firm handshake.

"Nice to meet you Gina. Lucas Jones. Steven has told me all about you."

Yeah and you've seen even more. "And you Lucas it's nice to put a face to the name."

"Hmm, yes, I've felt my ears burning over the past week or so." He smiles and his eyes wrinkle. I would place him in his mid-forties. His hair is greying and he is tanned. His clothes look expensive, which doesn't surprise me since apparently, he is an extremely proficient lawyer.

"It's been a little nuts since Leah turned up."

"That's what Lucas is here to talk about," Steven nods to Lucas.

"Well I've already told Steven this. I'm afraid it's not the best news but I have made a compromise so that we can keep Steven's name out of it. The producers of the show have agreed that Steven can give his DNA sample anonymously. They will let him know the results before the show airs and we can take it from there if need be, privately."

"But what if she uses his name? She can out him right away and she seems to really have some animosity towards him."

Lucas takes a sip of his coffee.

"Even if she does, they'll bleep it out. Like I said

153

it's not the best news but it's the best I can do. She has the right to do whatever she wants but she has been warned about naming Steven. I've managed to get a temporary interdict against Leah, which means if she does say anything and his name ends up out there, we can have her prosecuted. It's only in place for four weeks though. After the end date we can apply for another one if we need it."

This is a lot of information to take in, but I must admit, what Lucas is saying makes me feel better.

"So, when does the show get recorded then?"

"Friday."

I'm a little shocked that it's so soon. "Oh. Wow that's not giving much time to get the DNA sample to them."

Lucas holds up an envelope with address stickers all over it. "That's what this is for. I'm having this sent by courier to them this morning, so they'll have it on time. I think they throw a lot of money at getting these tests expedited so they'll have the result by the time they record the show."

"Okay, so my next question, when does it air?" I need this bullshit to be over; the sooner the better.

Lucas gets up from his seat. He's taller than I expected him to be. "They told me that they usually air within a week or so of recording, but we'll know the results as soon the show is recorded." He puts his hand on my shoulder. "I wish I could say it will be ok, but we really won't know until the results come back."

"I suppose it's just a waiting game now then?"

"Unfortunately yes. Guys I need to go, I've got a case calling at the Sheriff Court this afternoon. As soon as I get any information, I'll let you know."

"Thanks mate I'll walk you out," Steven says solemnly.

As they reach the living room door, Lucas stops and turns to me.

"Oh, and by the way, I have eyes in the audience, so we'll know more than just the results," he winks at me and I smile.

When Lucas is gone Steven joins me at the table in the kitchen. He looks pensive.

"You okay?"

He slumps down in the seat across from me. "I'm so sorry Gina. This is fucked up isn't it?"

"You could say that, but we don't really have much of a choice but to go with the flow, do we?"

"I can't believe how well you're taking all this."

I have to laugh at that. "Are you kidding? I'm a fucking mess inside Steven. I've spent so long putting on a front for people that I can do it whenever the need arises. I just want this all to be over. We don't need it."

Steven takes my hands on the table. "We'll get through this."

"I know we will. I love you Steven, please know I'll be here no matter what happens."

He squeezes my hands.

"So tell me, who does Lucas have going to Manchester for the show recording?"

"His wife. She's a big fan apparently."

"Nice," I say with a smile.

CHAPTER 19

I MUST HAVE READ every sign and poster on the walls in the main reception area of the Highland Hideaways head office twice. Above me are huge vaulted ceilings with large skylights. It is light and airy but warm and comforting at the same time. It's a new, modern building and the design is beautiful. I'm here for a meeting with Mr Johnson to discuss my photographs and I'm as nervous as hell. Steven has a meeting in Falkirk today so I decided to take the train to Edinburgh instead of using Gerry so I could collate some photos for Mr Johnson. I was so nervous, though, that I found myself staring at the screen for forty minutes or so and then it was almost time to get off.

I decided on a simple black shift dress and low heels. Trying to look professional, I put my hair in a chignon. I sincerely hope my makeup hasn't slid off my face. You can't look professional with panda eyes.

"Ms Harper?"

I look up at the mention of my name and am greeted by a very young, brown haired woman.

"I'm Susana. Mr Johnson is ready for you. If you would like to follow me."

I stand, smooth my dress, take a deep breath and try to compose myself.

We take an elevator up to the fourth floor and alight in a small reception area with some chairs and a desk holding only a computer and a phone.

"Okay, Ms Harper if you would like to take a seat, I'll let Mr Johnson know you're here."

I take a seat on one of three Wassily style chairs, which are actually very comfortable despite their tubular, industrial appearance. I'm in the middle of wondering whether they are expensive trademarked versions or copies when Susana reappears with Mr Johnson.

"Gina it's so good to see you again."

I stand and shake his hand. "You too Mr Johnson."

"Call me Ed, please? It makes me feel old when people call me Mr Johnson."

Susana laughs from behind her computer and Ed takes a pen from his trouser pocket and throws it at her. It misses her and she sniggers at him as we walk into his office.

"I'm telling mum," she laughs.

I like to see people having a good working relationship and it appears this one is kept in the family.

"Susana is my oldest daughter. She's filling in for my PA who is on maternity leave," he says, obviously wishing to explain their interaction. Before he closes the door, he winks at her. "Although her cheek is going to get her the sack."

He chuckles to himself as he closes the door. As I take a seat in front of the huge glass and wood desk, I notice a picture of Ed, a tall brunette woman and four brown haired girls of varying heights. *What a lovely family.* Susana obviously has the same type of fun relationship with her dad as I do with mine.

"Right Gina, let's get down to business." Ed takes his seat on the other side of the desk. "I loved what I saw at the exhibition and those photos of the Northern Lights are exactly what we are looking for to feature in our winter campaign this year. I actually started this company because of a trip my wife and I took on Lewis right after we got married. I fell in love with the highlands and islands and I realised how much we have on our doorstep that a lot of us natives don't even know about."

I nod. "Yes, I totally agree. I saw a lot from the plane that I didn't know existed and I was utterly blown away by Harris. I've never seen anything so beautiful or tranquil."

"It does take your breath away. Steven was fortunate to bag the land he built his house on. That part of Luskentyre is out of this world."

I can feel my brow furrow and Ed sees it. *I knew it.* I knew there was more to this. It was absolutely impossible that someone who owns a company like this just happened to come across the opening night of the exhibition I was in. I'm trying my hardest to stay calm, but I can feel tears pricking my eyes. Wonderful, I'm going to have a hissy fit and probably be escorted off the premises.

"Gina are you okay, you've gone a little pale?"

Ed looks genuinely concerned and I remember Ellen's words to me. '*Don't turn down any help.*' I take a shaky breath and nod.

"Yes, sorry Ed. This is a little overwhelming. I wasn't really expecting my work to get picked up like this."

It's not a lie but it's not the real reason for my mini meltdown. I can't help myself, I'm curious as to how he knows Steven. There's definitely more to it than simply an invitation to an art exhibition.

"Gina, my company has a reputation to keep. I wouldn't have asked for your work if I didn't think it was excellent."

"Thanks Ed, it means a lot to me that people like what I do. I'm really sorry to ask this but how do you know Steven?"

Ed sits back and clasps his hands in front of him. "Well this building we are in right now is how I met him. He was the architect on the project to build this office four years ago. We moved here to Leith from a tiny little office in the centre of Edinburgh when we started our international side of the business. We needed bigger offices and Steven won me over. He's a very talented guy, but you'll know that."

Hmm, do I ever! I nod. "Yeah he is. Did he ask you to come to the exhibition?"

Ed smiles. "Am I about to get him in trouble here?"

"Well that depends."

"I happened to bump into Steven about six months ago and during the conversation about how our businesses were going I mentioned that we'd be championing Scottish photographers to front our international campaigns. He contacted me at the start of February to tell me about the exhibition." Ed leans forward and puts his hands on the desk. "You're a talented artist Gina, Steven can see that. I didn't know you were his girlfriend until after we met at the exhibition. The only thing he said to me was that I should see the work on the opening night and gave me the Markham Ponsonby Gallery number to contact."

"So you're saying he only pointed you in the right direction?" I'm starting to feel slightly better.

"Absolutely. Listen, I don't do favours for people regardless of how well I know them. Ask Susana; I made her interview for the temporary PA position. Please know you did this on your own merits Gina."

"Thank you Ed, I really do appreciate this opportunity."

"So did you get a chance to have the contract looked over?"

Steven had Lucas look at the contract and he gave it the go ahead. "Yes I did and it's perfect." I pull the envelope from the back of my laptop bag and hand it to him.

"Wonderful Gina. I'm really happy to be working with you on this. Now, did you manage to put together any other photos we might be able to use?"

"I have a lot actually and I did try to do some work on the train, but it didn't quite happen. I have my laptop here, if you have a little time, I can show you them now."

"Go for it."

I get my laptop out and pull up my photo folder. Thankfully, I always arrange my photos into separate folders and label them all. Being a 'Monica' about this has finally paid off. I show him all my Harris pictures, well the PG ones, and leave the office with a sense of self-satisfaction. Ed has agreed to take thirty additional photos and four videos from me to be used in various formats for this year's winter advertising campaign. We went over the contract again to ensure that I knew how I would be paid. Ed gave me a lot of data to look at but right now my understanding is that every website click, booking and YouTube like generates me income.

After looking at the figures from last year I can see that I am about to make a small fortune working with this company. The set of photos will become the property of, and be used by, Highland Hideaways for the duration of the campaign and ownership will return to me at the end of it. This was one of the points that made me happy to sign the contract. These photos are special to me so I will be glad to have the rights to them back.

I step out of the building and back into the damp March air with a lovely feeling and a smile on my face. As I head towards the city centre to meet up with Charlie my phone rings. Seeing Steven's name makes my smile even wider.

"Hey handsome."

"Gina I've just heard from Lucas. The show was taped this morning and he has news for us. Are you done with your meeting?"

Oh shit! In my little business deal haze I completely forgot all about Leah's appearance on TV.

163

"Eh, yeah. I was supposed to be meeting Charlie, but I'll call her. I'll go straight for the train now."

"Stay where you are. I'm only twenty-five minutes away, I'll come and get you."

We hang up and I head into a little coffee shop next to Ed's office building. I buy a bottle of fresh orange juice and feel sick as I take a drink of it. My hands are shaking, I'm so terrified of what lies ahead.

CHAPTER 20

THE DRIVE FROM EDINBURGH to the lawyer's office has been nothing short of uncomfortable. Steven has managed to keep the conversation pinned to my meeting with Ed but there's been a feeling of apprehension in the air from both of us. I'm honestly scared to think about the consequences of what we are about to hear.

Lucas' office is on Bath Street and as Steven pulls up outside, I wish I was back in Edinburgh. Back in my little self-satisfied bubble. Given the fact that nothing seems to have gone right for us since we got together, I don't see this day ending well.

"I suppose it's now or never." Steven sounds as nervous as I feel.

"Mmhm," there's not really much I can say.

As I start to open my door, Steven grabs my arm.

"Gina," he closes his eyes and lets out a long sigh. Opening his eyes, he fixes me with a pained look. "Please know that I love you and no matter what happens here today I always will."

"Steven, what do you think is going to happen? Do you think I'm going to leave you if the boy is yours? Please, give me more credit than that." I place a reassuring hand on his. "I love you too, more than you know. We just need to take this step by step. Okay."

"Oh Gina. I'm so glad I have you to help me through this. I'm bricking it here."

"Let's go. Lucas will think we've done a runner."

Walking up the stairs to Lucas' office feels like a walk of the condemned. We are greeted by the receptionist who tells us to go straight through. She knows Steven well and I wonder how often he has needed to use Lucas' services. The office is bright and airy, and we find Lucas at his desk.

"Hi guys come in, take a seat."

We sit in the two seats on the other side of the desk and Steven takes my hand.

"I'm going to get right down to this if you don't mind. There is a lot to tell you." Lucas opens the folder sitting in front of him. "First things first, the boy is not your child Steven. DNA came back negative."

I feel Steven's body physically relax but I also see sadness in his eyes.

"Hey, are you ok?"

"Yeah. I'm fine. It's just a shock because she was so adamant it was me, I kind of got a little used to the idea."

"Well, this is the rest I have to tell you, or show you," Lucas directs our attention to the small TV on a long cabinet behind him.

"Do you have the recording already?" Steven asks, his eyes wide.

"Well, it's not the official recording, Nina managed to catch some of it on her phone."

"Lucas is that even legal?" I'm a little shocked but more intrigued.

He shrugs. "Nobody asked her for her phone. Are you ready for this?"

"Yes," we both say rather enthusiastically. We look at each other and smile.

As the footage starts it's a little jumpy and the microphone makes a scratchy sound. The camera focuses on the stage and we see Leah looking smug. She's talking animatedly to Jeremy Kyle, revelling in her 5 minutes of fame.

"So you're… how certain are you that this guy is the father?" Jeremy asks her as he starts to open the envelope he has in his hand.

"Oh, one hundred per cent and when it's proved I'll make sure he pays back money for Declan. I've done nothing but care for my son since he was born with no help from anyone." Her voice is venomous, and I want to punch the fucking screen.

"Did you tell this man he was a dad when you found out you were pregnant or when Declan was born?"

She looks flustered and a bit embarrassed. "Well…no…but that's not the point."

The audience boos and she looks like she might blow a fuse.

Jeremy shakes his head. "Right let's see what these results say. So," he takes the card out of the envelope, "how certain were you?"

"More than a hundred per cent."

"Hmm, he's not Declan's father."

I'm expecting her to dispute the fact or at least go nuts that the result wasn't what she wanted but her reaction shocks me. She shrugs her shoulders and says, "Oh well it was worth a try."

Steven looks at me with wide eyes and pure fury on his face. I have to admit I am rather furious myself. She put us through all this heartache and worry knowing full well the kid wasn't even be Steven's. We both look back at the screen as the audience boos louder and Jeremy berates her for wasting his time.

"What did you say? '*It was worth a try*'. Was this guy ever really a potential dad or did you just pluck him out of thin air?"

Leah smiles as if it's all a bloody joke. "Well the other guy is a worthless piece of shit and he's got no money, so this one was the best bet."

Jeremy looks like he's about to pop a vein. "Answer the question," he demands.

Finally, she looks defeated and the smug smile starts to fade. "No, he wasn't," she mumbles looking at her hands.

My blood is boiling and I realise I am clenching my fist so hard that my nails are digging into my palms. Jeremy sits down beside Leah.

"Why would you do that to someone? Why would you do that to your son?"

She shrugs her shoulders again. "Cos he's got money and lots of it. He won't miss it."

"You know love, people like you make me sick. Do you realise what that can do to a child? To be used like that, for your own gain. It's disgusting."

"My son is fine, I love my son."

"Then why not tell the truth. Once this show airs it's out there, he will see this at some point in his life."

Leah smiles. "It was only the money I wanted. I wouldn't let my son watch your shit show anyway. I'm better than you," she mumbles.

The audience gasps collectively and a few more boos are thrown her way.

"So you think it's okay to blackmail someone because they have done well for themselves and you haven't? That's despicable."

"Don't really care. He's got his new family so he wouldn't have cared about Declan anyway."

"You're a disgusting piece of work young lady. I honestly don't think I want you on this stage anymore. Off you go."

Leah stands up and the audience boos again. She turns to them and sticks her middle finger up.

"Fuck you," she shouts as she walks off.

The recording goes wonky as it ends and the screen goes blank. There is silence between the three of us. I look to Steven and he shakes his head.

Lucas breaks the silence. "Guys, I'm sorry you had to go through all this. I really wasn't expecting this outcome."

"I…" Steven lets go of my hand and stands. He starts pacing, clenching and unclenching his fists and I can see he's angry.

"Fucking little bitch."

I go to him and put my hand on his shoulder. I'm a little shocked when he shrugs me off. I sit down a little hurt and I can see Lucas looks uncomfortable.

"What do we do now Lucas?" Steven demands.

I can't think of anything to say. The air is thick with tension and I'm close to tears.

"Well, there isn't really anything else to do. The DNA test was negative and Leah has been exposed as a liar. I also managed to get hold of this."

Lucas hands me a plastic folder containing what looks like a birth certificate. It's not like any I've seen before. It's an English one and the registration district is shown as Cambridgeshire. As I scan the rest of the information, I'm surprised to see that it is a copy of Declan's birth certificate.

"How did you get this?"

He leans back in his chair. "Birth records are public. All you need is the right information and you can get any certificate you want. It took a little bit of research, but I eventually managed to find what I needed."

Steven sits back down beside me.

"When did you and Leah break up?" I ask him.

"Ehm, it would have been eight or so years ago, 2009, I think. Yeah it was. The middle of December 2009."

As I read further down the birth certificate the date of birth shows me what a horrible, deceitful bitch Leah really is. Declan was born on the thirtieth of December two thousand and ten. A full year after she dumped Steven.

"That fucking nasty bitch. She knew all along Declan wasn't your child."

Steven's face is like thunder and I don't blame him in the least. "You know, I really don't care about what she's done to me, it's that kid I feel angry for. What sort of mother does that to her child?"

He rests his elbows on the desk and puts his head in his hands. I get why he is so angry. Steven has enormous empathy with children whose parents use them for their own gain. He suffered as a child and he hates to see other children suffer, at the hands of their parents especially.

I put my hand on his shoulder and feel him relax a little. This time he doesn't flinch away from me.

"Steven, I know this is going to sound insensitive, but you don't have anything to do with this anymore. Leah has no ties to you at all." Lucas gives me a reassuring look.

Steven sits back. "I know and thank you Lucas; you and Nina. I suppose we can't save all the children in the world can we?" He gives me a defeated look.

"I think it's time we went home. I honestly don't think I can take much more stress right now and I certainly know you can't."

We leave Lucas' office and are greeted with pouring rain and darkening skies fitting our mood perfectly. Making a run for the car doesn't help, we end up soaked by the time we eventually get into our seats. We are both breathing heavily and I start laughing as water runs down my forehead.

Steven reaches over and wipes it with his thumb. His eyes turn all at once fiery and he kisses me with such determination that I can do nothing else but succumb. I gasp for air when he releases my lips.

"Let's get out of here, I need to get you naked and this car's not big enough."

The car roars to life and I sit back with a smile on my face. *Finally something going in our favour*, I think to myself as Steven speeds the car through the busy streets of the city centre.

CHAPTER 21

"DAD AND I ARE so proud of you Gina. Both you and Steven. This charity is going to be amazing," Mum sips her coffee as we both sit at the kitchen table. "This place is beautiful Gina, it's not what I expected a '*bachelor pad*' to look like." She air quotes the bachelor pad bit.

"What did you think it would look like, empty pizza boxes and lager cans?"

"No, I mean the décor. If it were left to your dad our whole house would look like his office. Dark wood panelling, dark carpet and no sunlight. I swear I sometimes think he goes in there to turn into a vampire. When he's not home I open the blinds. Makes me feel dangerous," she laughs.

"To be honest, I think Steven had an interior decorator do this place. Come to think of it, he seems to have people to do most things for him."

"Are you still finding all this a bit overwhelming honey?"

I let out a long sigh. "Yeah, a little. I really thought we were getting on track and starting to actually enjoy being a couple. Then Leah had to come on the scene and ruin it. Honestly mum, I'm ready for all this drama to be over."

Mum puts her hand on mine; it's warm from her coffee cup.

"Oh darling, you know things don't always run smoothly in relationships. I'll tell you dad and I had our fair share of drama when we were first together. Okay, so it wasn't '*Gina and Steven*' drama but it was drama to us."

"What happened?"

"Well, the first house we bought together was a tiny ground floor flat. We were both still students and it cost us an arm and a leg. We managed to get the place decorated and it looked lovely. I was so proud of it." She looks pained as she talks. "The neighbour right upstairs was a guy in his fifties whose family had disowned him because of his alcohol addiction. He was a nice enough guy though. Kept himself to himself and never caused us any trouble. Anyway, one night we had gone to a wedding and stayed overnight at the hotel. When we arrived back home in the morning the building was in complete chaos. Apparently the guy upstairs had gone for a bath, got in with the taps still running, had a heart attack, drowned and flooded everything down stairs. Our beautiful little flat was ruined."

"Oh mum, that's terrible."

"Yes his family were pretty cut up about the fact that they'd disowned him and then he died like that, all alone. What made it worse for us was that we only had insurance for the house, not the contents. It was stupid but we were poor and couldn't afford it. The water had been running until four in the morning. It was only because one of the other neighbours was coming home from work in a night club that it was noticed."

"God, that is drama."

"Yeah, and the next one went on fire. All we needed was famine and pestilence and we'd have our own wee apocalypse. Obviously it pales in comparison with everything that's happened to you. It was quite traumatic at the time for us though. You know it doesn't matter what happens in your life, it's how you cope and move on that matters."

"I know, it just seems as though there is some unknown force that doesn't want us to be together." I laugh at myself because I can hear how crazy I sound.

"Sweetheart you'll be fine, you're stronger than you know. So, tell me more about this charity. I can't think of a better use for your money and dad and I will help you out as much as we can."

"Oh mum, it's amazing but daunting at the same time. I've never run a charity before, I don't have the first clue about what I'm doing."

"I'm sure Steven will have a team of people ready to help you. Now let me see your plans."

**

"Well hello lovey ladies," Steven croons.

"Christ almighty where did you come from?" Mum looks at Steven with wide eyes and I can't help myself but laugh.

"Sorry, Carla, I thought you heard me come in," Steven laughs. "Are you okay?"

"Barely, I'm glad this mug was empty," she holds her coffee cup up and shakes her head.

"What are you up to?" Steven asks as he kisses the top of my head.

"I've been showing mum our plans for the charity. She's been giving me some great advice on fundraising."

Mum nods. "You two have a great model here. There's going to be some very appreciative kids out there once this gets up and running."

"It was Gina's idea. She's utterly amazing."

"Well, she's my daughter so that's a given," mum

laughs at her own joke. "Right, sweetheart, I'm going to head home. Ruth, Denise and I are off to a dinner party at Sheila's tonight. Do you remember Sheila? That was her who married the football manager. Thinks she's like the rest of the WAG's now and talks with a stupid posh accent but forgets we all knew her at school," she rolls her eyes.

"Do you need a lift Carla? I can get Gerry to take you home."

"Oh, thanks son, but I'm going to try and find something to wear that's befitting of Sheila's mansion. I honestly wonder why I'm still friends with that woman." She hugs us both and heads out the door singing to herself. Steven stares at the door.

"Are you ok?"

He turns to me and smiles. "I love your family Gina. The way your mum talked to me there, it…" he trails off and shakes his head. "It's just nice to belong."

"Oh, Steven, my parents think the world of you." I rub his arm. "They know you love me and that's all that matters to them."

He turns and lifts me off my feet. "I do love you, with all my heart Gina. More than you'll ever know." Placing me back on the floor he kisses me softly. "I have something for you."

"Ooh really?"

"Come with me."

He takes my hand and leads me to the TV room. In the middle of the snooker table is a huge black box trimmed with white. The black satin ribbon tied around it has white writing on it, as does the box lid. I gasp. Oscar de la Renta! When I look questioningly at Steven he nods. I pull off the ribbon, which is so luxurious it could be a garment on its own, and open the top of the box. The white tissue paper is monogrammed with the designer logo. I pull out the dress inside. It is plain black with long sleeves and is scalloped on one shoulder. I love it so much, but I know for a fact that this probably cost the same as three sets of wedding photographs.

"Steven this is so beautiful but really it's too much. I…" I'm shut down by a kiss and it is soft and slow and bewitching.

"I would buy you the moon if I could, Gina," Steven whispers against my lips.

"Thank you," I concede.

"That's better." He slowly pulls my skirt up to my waist and lifts me onto the purple baize of the snooker table. He carefully puts my dress back in the box then moves the whole lot to the sofa.

"Move into the middle of the table," he says with his back to me. I do as I'm ordered and prop myself up on my elbows. I watch his back muscles flex as he removes his shirt and kicks off his shoes and I swear it is the best view in the world right now. He comes to the table and in one swift move he jumps up to straddle my thighs. He unbuttons my shirt just enough to get his hand into my bra and has me writhing under him when he pinches my nipple.

"Use me," he says as he moves beside me.

"What?" I'm confused.

He holds his hand up.

"Use me, make yourself come."

He knows exactly how to work me with his tone. I take his hand and push it inside my knickers. It should feel awkward and probably would have five months ago but now it feels so right. Now I feel less inhibited, thanks to Steven. He has changed me in ways I never thought possible, taught me things about myself I never would have found out on my own.

"God you feel so good Gina."

I guide his finger inside me and press on the heel of his hand against my clit and so help me I don't even last five seconds before my body is firing off. I can't stop; my orgasm just keeps coming and coming. I let out a guttural moan as Steven withdraws his hand and pulls on the delicate lace of my thong. The snap of the elastic makes me gasp and before I can comprehend what's happened, he thrusts himself inside me and I feel my bum cheeks rub on the surface of the table. Obviously sympathetic to the little baize burn situation

I have going on he puts his hands on my bum and uses it go get deeper. It doesn't take him long to come either and as the high subsides we both stay still, breathing heavily and staring at each other.

"Well that was a first. Never been fucked at snooker before," I smile.

Steven laughs and leans down to kiss me. "Wear that dress tonight and underwear is not an option."

CHAPTER 22

BLACK IS FULL TO bursting tonight. Saturdays are usually busy but tonight there is a special act on, and it seems most of the club's members and their significant others are here. I saw the poster boards in the entrance and I'm so excited. The act is a couple of former professional ballroom dancers who were once the best in the world. I love ballroom dancing. I used to love sitting with mum watching 'Come Dancing'. I loved all the beautiful costumes they wore and always wanted to be one of them. I even talked mum into letting me try it out. I got about four lessons in and quit. The teacher was a complete cow and used to shout at anyone who didn't get the steps right. I was only eight years old, so I took it badly when I got yelled at. I went home crying that day and never went back. It didn't stop me watching programmes on TV with total fascination though. Now it's 'Strictly Come Dancing', or 'Dancing with the Stars' if you're American. The couple performing tonight did a stint on 'Come Dancing' in the late 90's and then went on to dominate the world.

"I can't wait to see this," Cerys is already a little tipsy.

Steven and I are on a night out with Charlie and Mark and Cerys and her partner Amanda. It's the first time I've met her and she's just as nice as Cerys. This is just what we needed after the week we've had.

"Yeah she's talked about nothing else since she found out they were going to be here," Amanda rolls her eyes at Cerys and they both start laughing.

"Well, I love ballroom dancing. I would have loved to do that, but my mum wanted me to be a figure skater. She was one of those pushy parents and because she did it when she was a lass, she thought I should too," Cerys turns to Amanda and tips her head to the side. "And you wonder why I don't talk to her anymore."

I look to Steven and he gives me the slightest shake of his head. He has already told me that Cerys was kicked out at nineteen when she came out to her family. I was shocked and I think it's one of the reasons why Steven can relate to her so well. I count myself extremely lucky that my parents loved and nurtured me when I was growing up and I appreciate them even more since I met Steven.

"So how did you two get together then?" Charlie asks Cerys and Amanda.

They smile at each other and then end up in full blown hysterics.

"Ehm," Amanda starts then looks to Cerys. "You tell them."

"Okay. So, when I moved to Glasgow, I managed to bag myself a great little house in a nice area just outside the city. It was a rented property, so the landlords did all the maintenance and stuff." Cerys looks at Amanda and laughs again. "Oh fuck it, she was my window cleaner alright."

The whole table erupts in laughter. These two obviously get a kick out of telling this story and I can see why.

"So did you catch her spying on you?" Charlie asks Cerys.

"I could lie and tell you that's how it happened, but it was more like something out of a Carry On movie," Cerys laughs.

"Yeah, this twit knocked me off my ladder. Broke my bloody squeegee."

"Oh my God how the hell did you manage that?" Charlie is getting sucked right in to this story. I think she's enjoying having some adult conversation.

"I was on my way down the ladder after doing the

upstairs windows and she opened the upstairs window that the ladder was leaning on."

Cerys holds her hand up. "In my defence, I had only just moved in and didn't even know there was a window cleaner. I thought someone was trying to break in."

Steven and Mark are sitting watching the conversation going back and forth and I can tell by the look on Steven's face that he has heard this story more than once.

"I only fell about a metre onto the grass, but my good squeegee hit the concrete slabs and broke the handle clean off. I was so angry and I was ready to read the riot act when this appeared in front of me," Amanda gestures to Cerys. "I was hooked as soon as I saw her." She takes Cerys' hand. "I'm glad you almost killed me."

Everyone laughs as the lights dim and the dance floor is flooded with multi coloured lights. As the dancers walk onto the stage, I know exactly which dance they are going to perform from their attire. The man is wearing black dress trousers and his charcoal shirt looks like it is made out of lycra. His tie is thin and jet-black like his slicked back hair. The woman is draped in a charcoal lace dress with long sleeves and slits in the skirt.

The Argentine Tango is one of my favourite

dances. It's so dramatic and sexy and any time I've watched it in person or on TV I instantly feel transported to a small informal club in Buenos Aires. This night is no different. The lighting creates a feeling of intimacy and it's as though we are right there in the moment with the dancers. They start their dance and I am mesmerised by their footwork. It's so fast and intricate and by normal standards they should be falling over each other. I certainly would. How they manage to do this is beyond me. I sit and watch them in absolute awe and a tiny piece of me wishes I hadn't given up my lessons so easily.

***

The night winds to a close and we get ready to leave the club, but Cerys is a bit worse for wear. She really has drunk far too much, and I can see that Amanda is a little pissed at her.

"There's a taxi waiting outside for you both Amanda. Mark and I will help her out ok."

Steven looks to Mark who nods and they both get an arm each over their shoulder and make her walk.

"Steven, please don't fire me," she mumbles.

"Oh shut up you big lush. I'll never find anyone else I can rip the piss out of."

I laugh as Charlie, Amanda and I follow on behind them. Poor Amanda looks like she wants the ground to open up and swallow her.

"Hey are you okay?" I ask.

"Och I'm fine. She doesn't normally drink like this. I think she was nervous about us all being out together. She really likes you Gina. She told me how much happier Steven is since he met you, and my God the amount of stuff you've been through already you both deserve a medal. She'll be all apologetic tomorrow and she won't drink like that again until she has her next internal crisis," Amanda rolls her eyes and gives a half-hearted smile.

We are last to exit the club and Steven and Mark get Cerys into the back of the taxi. Amanda thanks them and gives Steven a little kiss on the cheek before getting in with her.

"Ooh is she in for a ribbing on Monday morning," Steven laughs.

I'm about to ask where Gerry is to take us home when the man himself appears at the kerb in the Range Rover. As we move towards the car there's a commotion behind us and a familiar voice screeches above the din.

"Steven you fucking bastard I'm going to fucking kill you."

Everyone looks in Leah's direction and the next ten seconds seem to happen in slow motion. Leah heads straight towards Steven with a kitchen knife in her hand. She is screaming like a woman possessed and I freeze unable to move. I watch in utter amazement as Charlie gets down on her knees and rugby tackles Leah to the ground. She loses her grip on the knife and Charlie sits on top of her, grabbing her wrists and holding them above her head.

"Someone phone the police," shouts Charlie.

"I'm on it," Steven shouts back to her.

Mark looks like he's seen a ghost, but I swear I can see a little bit of pride in his expression. I give myself a mental shake and kneel down beside Charlie and Leah.

"What are you doing Leah?"

"Fuck you Gina. You've got the perfect life, the baby *and* the man. I've got fuck all," she bears her teeth in a sneer. "I fucking hate you," she screams.

"For fuck sake Leah that baby wasn't ours. Why are you doing this? You have a son to take care of."

I'm taken aback when Leah starts to cry, really hard sobbing crying. "He took Declan away from me."

I'm about to ask what she's talking about but the arrival of the police and their blues and two's interrupts and the crowd that had gathered around us starts to disperse.

I feel Steven's heat behind me and he lifts me up. A female police officer gets Charlie up off Leah and the male officer hoists Leah up and takes her to the back of the police car. She goes willingly and despite myself I feel sorry for her.

The female officer comes to talk to us. "Can you guys stay here so that my colleagues can get your statements?"

"Sure, we'll wait in the club," Steven ushers us all back inside. "Gerry I'll call you tomorrow, we'll get a taxi home. Thanks mate," Gerry nods and gets back in the car.

Charlie and Mark are in front of us in the corridor and Steven gives a little laugh. "Hey Ronda Rousey, take the keys and wait in my office."

Charlie turns and smacks him on the arm. "You should be thanking me; I saved your life tonight. That head case was going to murder you and I couldn't let her bury another man. What kind of friend would I have been? Fucking bitch made me rip my tights."

"Thanks Charlie, I really do appreciate it," Steven hands her the keys. "We won't be long. I'll get us some drinks."

I watch them walk through the doors towards the office and as the door closes, I lean my back against the cool wall and let out a sigh.

Steven puts his hands on my waist. "Are you okay?"

"Oh Steven when is this ever going to end? I was just saying to mum this morning that I was ready for all this drama to be over. You couldn't make this shit up."

Steven sighs and shakes his head. "Sometimes I wonder if your life would be better if we had never met. I should have left you alone. You almost died because of me."

I shake my head and put my arms round his neck. "I really hate to admit this but at one point I thought the same, but you know what Steven, I wouldn't change meeting you for the world. You've given me a reason to get up in the morning. Before I met you I was wasting my life wallowing in grief. You've enlightened me to the fact that my life isn't over and I love you for it." I put my hand on his cheek feeling the light stubble. "You're the best thing that's ever happened to me. I trust you completely and I know you love me."

His answering kiss is full of love and an unspoken promise to never let me go.

"You look amazing tonight," he whispers against my lips. "I'm never going to stop loving you Gina, even when we're old and wrinkly, I'll always love you."

"I love you too Steven, now let's get some drinks and go and join Charlie and Mark. The police will be here soon and then I'd really like to get home. I'm exhausted."

Steven takes my hand and we walk towards the bar. He rubs my knuckles and I smile. I love this man and I know we will be absolutely fine. Our short relationship has survived more than most couples go through in their entire lives. I think he's right, no matter what happens, we'll be fine.

CHAPTER 23

"IT'S A RUBBER PLANT."

"Huh?" Nate's voice startles me.

"You were telling me about what happened on Saturday night then just stopped talking. You've been stroking that leaf for about five minutes."

"Oh God, I'm sorry Nate. I know your time is precious."

"It's okay Gina, this is what I'm here for. You were on a roll and then you went a little glassy eyed and contemplative."

"I know. Steven and I have had quite a bit to talk about since Saturday night. This thing with Leah runs much deeper than trying to pin the kid on Steven. We've since found out that she really hasn't had the best time since she left the UK for America all those years ago. Just knowing her story and what she's been through makes me feel sorry for her. I should hate her for what she put Steven through, but I don't."

"Interesting," Nate writes something down in his notebook. "You say '*what she put Steven through.*' Do you not feel that she put you through anything?"

"Well, not really."

"Why not?"

"Emmm...Because it was all about Steven."

He nods. "Okay, and are you in a relationship with Steven?"

"Yes, what are you getting at?"

"You live with each other, you're going to be working together and as I remember you telling me last week she got personal with you when you first met."

"Yes but..."

"So by my reckoning, and I dare say anyone else who's heard this story, you went through as much as Steven."

I think about that for a second. Maybe he's right. I didn't really think it was my place to feel violated by Leah. It wasn't about me, but seeing me with Georgie that day probably made things a whole lot worse.

"Okay, yes, I suppose you're right."

"So how do you feel about that?"

"I don't know. Pissed off I suppose," I shake my head and look at my hands in my lap.

"You've come a long way in the last four months

Gina. You're a strong woman and you've been through more than anyone should have to deal with. Do you feel like it has changed your relationship at all?"

"Maybe, if anything it's made us stronger. I feel like we've become a team," I laugh and shake my head. "I don't mean to sound clichéd but it's the only way I can describe it."

Nate nods, a knowing smile on his face.

I get it, finally. "Okay you win, we did go through all this together."

"Gina it's not about me winning. You go from one extreme to the other. On one hand you want to take on the world and your problems all by yourself and on the other, you want to fight other people's battles for them. You need to remember that a problem shared is a problem halved."

I know he's right. "I don't know why I do that. I think it's a guilt thing to be honest."

"What do you mean?"

"When I found out about Steven's life when he was a kid, I felt so guilty. I had a picture perfect upbringing and I thought it wasn't fair."

"And that's the reason behind the charity?"

"Yes but now, talking to you, I think I'm doing it for the wrong reasons. I'm so confused."

"I don't think it's for the wrong reasons Gina, but I don't think you need to feel guilty for something that wasn't and isn't your fault. You're not omnipotent. You can't change every bad thing that happens in the world. I think what you and Steven are doing is nothing short of amazing and I know how much it is going to benefit disadvantaged children. I also know how immensely proud Steven is of you."

This makes me smile. "I'm proud of him too. He's started being more open with me and trying not to hide things from me to protect me. I told him he needed to stop trying to do every… thing… him…self. Oh."

Nate's smile gets wider. "There it is. Live by your own advice Gina. Stop trying to do everything yourself, it'll only backfire on you."

"I hate it that you're right all the time."

"I don't get paid to be wrong, you should know that by now."

I laugh at him as I stand to leave. These sessions have changed so much since I found out about Aiden's affair. Nate has helped me with so many things going on in my life other than my grief and I feel bad for dismissing therapy in the first place. I treated it like it was a chore when in reality, it has more or less given me back my life.

"Gina I would like to see you and Steven together at some point this week. I was going to talk to him about this last week, but he buggered off so quickly after our session that I didn't get a chance. You both need to talk about what happened with Colin."

The mention of that name makes me shudder. Shaking my head, I close my eyes against the onslaught of emotion it evokes in me. "We have talked about it," I whisper.

"Gina look at me"

I open my eyes and Nate gives me a reassuring nod.

"Yes you have talked about it, to me. You haven't spoken about it enough together."

He's right. Any time the subject comes up one or both of us shuts it down. It has become a bit of a taboo subject for us and I know it's not healthy. I just want Steven to stop hurting over it.

"You're right I know you are. When are you free to see us?"

"Tomorrow morning, all morning. Schedule it with Fiona and let Steven know."

I nod. "Thanks Nate. I guess we'll see you tomorrow then."

"See you then. Bye Gina."

I close the door behind me and steel myself as an all too familiar panic rises in my chest. I steady my breathing using the techniques Nate taught me. I've had less need to use these lately but knowing that I have to talk about my ordeal again and knowing how much it is going to hurt Steven makes me grateful that Nate imparted this knowledge to me.

***

The apartment is quiet when I get back from seeing Nate. I know Steven had a meeting with his building company this afternoon, so I assume it has run on a bit longer than he was expecting. I kick off my heels and head into the kitchen to make a coffee. The place is eerie when I'm here on my own. I wonder how Steven felt being here alone for so long. I notice a manila folder on the kitchen table. It's the same as the one Lucas used when we were at his office talking about Leah. There's a bright orange Post-It on the front.

Lucas sent this over. It's all the information he has on Leah.

A warm smile spreads across my face. Steven has left this for me. I make myself a coffee and sit at the table. I sip some and open the file.

There are a lot of single sheets of paper inside including the birth certificate Lucas showed us. Since we last saw Lucas, we have learned quite a bit about what has happened to Leah. She left America when she found out she was pregnant and ended up in England. The guy she was with tried to get her to terminate the pregnancy, but she had the baby in the UK. Somehow, she ended up back with him and after six months he won custody of Declan by claiming she was a neglectful mother. He threw Leah out of his apartment and she was only allowed visitation every other weekend and never an overnight. She spent years trying to get full custody back and disappeared at Christmas when she had been allowed to bring Declan over to the UK to visit her mum who was ill and dying. Shortly after her mother passed away, she had a mental breakdown and that's when she involved Steven in the mix. It seems she thought, in some sort of warped way, the DNA would come back positive for Steven and she would get money from him. Once she got it, she was going to make sure she and Declan disappeared.

As I wade through the file, I come across facts that start to put everything into perspective. From what I can gather Declan's dad was abusive, but nothing could be done about it due to lack of evidence. This all happened when she was pregnant, and it looks like he wore her down until she was forced to come back to him. He didn't want her; he was only interested in the child and the financial benefits he would bring. No wonder she went into downward spiral. There's only so much the human psyche can take before something's got to give. The further I read the worse I feel for her.

"Gina?"

My heart leaps at Steven's voice. "In the kitchen."

I hear him walk through the lounge and feel the hairs on my arms stand to attention as he reaches out to me. He kisses the top of my head. I lean back to look up at him and he kisses my lips.

"You've no idea how nice it is to come home to you."

"Yes, I do."

"Did you read all that?" He points at the folder.

"Most of it."

He walks over to the cupboard and pours himself a whisky. "What do you think? It's fucking tragic if you ask me."

"Yeah, I think so too. Is she getting help?"

"She's been admitted to a psychiatric hospital and she has a lawyer to deal with all her personal family problems. I she ever wants to stand a chance of getting her son back, her mental health is the most important thing she can work on right now. Lawyers love to exploit people's mental health issues."

I know he's right and I shake off the horrible feeling of knowing that's exactly what Lucas would have done to her had that boy been Steven's child.

"Did you help her Steven?" I know the answer to this question even before I ask it. He is such a caring guy and it's one of the many things I love about him. He sits down at the table and takes a drink of his whisky.

"I had to Gina. After hearing what she'd been through I felt dreadful for her."

"I do too."

"She fought for years to get her boy back from this abusive bastard who had, and still has, everyone fooled."

I shake my head. "I don't know why people feel like it's their right to be so nasty and controlling towards their partner. If you ever treated me like that I'd... let's just say I wouldn't let you treat me like that."

He smiles.

"I believe that and please know I'll never do anything other than love you."

"Well, hopefully now she'll get the help she needs, and her son will hopefully have a better life instead of being pushed from pillar to post."

"Hmm." He takes another drink of whisky as he closes the folder and moves it to the side. I take it as my cue to tell him about our therapy session tomorrow.

"Steven, Nate wants us both to go and see him tomorrow."

"Oh. Should I be worried?"

"That depends how you want to look at it. He wants to talk about Colin."

As soon as I mention his name the air between us shifts. I know this is going to be hard for him. Colin could have done anything to Steven and he would have dealt with it in his own strong and sure way but as soon as he involved me that all changed. His control was taken away when I was abducted and Steven knew better than anyone what Colin was capable of. He hasn't really ever spoken about how he felt when I was gone or how he felt when he found out Colin had died in the crash. He takes a deep breath and nods.

"I suppose this had to happen sooner or later. I know we should have aired all this as soon as you were back on your feet but I…" he pauses, puts his glass on the table and pulls me into his embrace. "I didn't want you to have to relive that shit over and over again," he whispers against my hair.

I lean back to look at him and see a pain behind his beautiful blue eyes. It hurts my heart and I know it will help to talk about it especially with Nate. We would never get through a full conversation together on our own. We won't have the option of changing the subject with Nate there to guide us.

"Nate will help us Steven. Let's just say the worst has already happened. Colin can't hurt us anymore and we've already proven we are stronger than that."

"I'm so glad you came into my life Gina. I love you." He kisses my forehead and smiles. "Permission to change the subject until tomorrow?"

"Of course," I nod.

"Okay what are we doing for dinner tonight then, it's getting late? Gerry says we have to be at the theatre for seven."

"Chinese? But I want to eat here."

"Great, we'll order in."

"Naked," I wink at him. I have actually mastered a wink now.

"Oh, you naughty girl," he downs the whisky and lifts me out of the chair. "The food can wait."

CHAPTER 24

"GINA YOU READY BABE?" Steven's voice echoes up the stairs.

"Down in a minute," I shout back as I put my earrings in.

It's early evening and we are going to The Theatre Royal to see a special young lady dancing with her dance school. Gerry's daughter, Laura, is that special young lady and when he told us about the show I could tell how proud he was. It's a showcase of all the different types of dance they do in the school. I actually think it's more of a '*this is what we do, please sign up to our school*' kind of night and I'm hoping it'll take my mind off what's to come at our therapy session tomorrow.

I grab my clutch bag and jacket and head down the stairs. Steven is sitting on the piano stool clinking the keys mindlessly with one hand while he reads something on his phone. He looks up and nods his appreciation.

"You look wonderful."

And so does he, but then he always does.

"Hey handsome," I swing my arms round his neck and kiss him.

"We need to leave now. We're slumming it tonight. Obviously Gerry can't drive us so we're taking the Aston."

Oh, I love that car.

"When's the last time you drove a car?"

I wasn't expecting that. This apartment is within walking distance or a short taxi ride to wherever we need to go, and we have Gerry for everything else.

"I don't know, before Christmas I suppose. Why?"

"That's too long. Here," he hands me the car key. "You're driving us tonight."

"Oh my God no Steven. I can't drive that car what if I have an accident. It's far too powerful for me." I am shaking holding onto the keys.

"Gina you'll be fine. Once you learn to drive you can drive almost anything. This car is a dream to drive, believe me."

I look down at my feet. I've never liked to drive in heels and these three inchers just won't do.

"Okay, let me get some flat shoes though."

"That's my girl," he slaps my bum as I start up the stairs and when I turn to him, he gives me that, oh so sexy wink.

***

I push the sapphire crystal key into the centre console of the car and the engine roars to life. The car rumbles beneath us and I'm so excited but truly shitting myself to be behind the wheel of this magnificent machine. I look to Steven who gives me a reassuring nod. I adjust my seat and start to drive away from the kerb, my hands gripping the steering wheel so tight my knuckles are white.

Steven puts his hand on mine. "Loosen your grip and just think of this as any other car you've driven. We have a bit of extra time before the show starts, why don't we take a spin on the motorway. Really let you try it out."

"Oh, I don't know Steven…"

"I dare you," he cuts me off. His voice is low and commanding.

"Ok." I take us west and onto the main road towards Charing Cross where we can join the M8 motorway. Because I'm starting to get a feel for the car, I give a little rev of the engine at the traffic lights. I look at Steven who has a smug look on his face.

"Feels good doesn't it?"

The light turns green. "Oh fuck yeah."

Since there is nothing in front of us, I press the accelerator and we speed off towards the motorway slip road.

"That's what I was looking for," Steven gives me a thumbs up as we enter the motorway traffic.

I check the mirrors and head across three lanes in one manoeuvre, getting into the fast lane as quickly as I can. I can feel the adrenaline racing through my body as I watch the speedometer rising.

"We can come off at the airport, there's plenty of roundabouts there to take us straight back on the motorway again."

"Mhm," I nod but I have no intention of coming off there. The part of the motorway we are on is quite busy because it is the main route to the airport but past that it is a little less congested so I know I can open this car up and really feel the force of it. I can feel Steven's eyes on me as we approach the slip road for Glasgow Airport. I'm in the wrong lane to come off and as I take the car a touch above seventy, he is left in no doubt about my intentions.

"Living dangerously Gina? I like it," his words have a slightly edgy undertone and I wonder if this is getting him as high as me.

I don't answer him, I simply smile and as soon as the traffic has thinned out, I boot the accelerator and we speed down the motorway. Steven has music playing low in the background and I recognise the singer. The song that has just started has a rocky uplifting beat to it and as we approach the start of the Erskine Bridge, I turn it up loud and push the car faster. I am driving at a ridiculously illegal speed now but somehow, I don't care. I feel free and my God do I feel good. I had no idea I could drive like this. VW Golfs and Ford Fiestas just don't have this kind of punch.

Steven is quiet as we leave the bridge and head back towards Glasgow. I have to slow down since this road is a little busier and as I do the realisation of what I've just done hits me like a brick and I long for a lay-by so that I can stop. The first place I come across is a hotel car park. I pull the car in and stop across two spaces.

As I turn off the ignition, I look at Steven who is sitting smiling at me. I wonder if this is what it feels like coming down from some intense drug induced high. I think I'm in shock.

"You okay."

"Oh my God," I put my hand on my chest and feel my heart going ten to the dozen.

"Fuck me Gina, you're shaking," he grabs my hand and rubs it hard.

"That was intense. I'm so sorry Steven. You should never have let me drive this," I close my eyes and

207

shake my head. "I could have killed us."

"Gina, you handled that like a pro. I didn't feel like we were in danger at all," he leans right across the centre console and pulls me into a hard kiss, his lips bruising mine. "I really want to take you home, but Gerry would kill us if we missed this."

I let out a long breath against his lips. "Can you drive? I think I'm going to have a heart attack here."

***

We have seats in the dress circle of the theatre. They are absolutely perfect because we can see the whole stage. Gerry and Julie ex-wife were already here when we arrived, and I've just finished recounting my driving experience to them.

"Are you crazy man? Imagine letting a woman drive that beautiful machine," Gerry laughs and is swiftly slapped on the arm by Julie.

"Ya cheeky sexist pig."

"I'm kidding, I'm kidding."

I'm about to pitch in and defend myself when the lights go down and the curtain goes up. There is a lot of tiny voices chitter chatting and girly giggling in the dark and when the stage lights go up, we hear a collective 'aww' from the audience. On the stage stand about twenty tiny little girls all dressed in aqua and white leotards with flowers of the same colour in their hair. They are all sparkly with glitter in their hair and on their faces. My heart is about to burst looking at how cute they all are.

As the music starts, they all move at the same time and jump around to a really fast paced song. I am exhausted just watching them.

The dancers all perform one by one in groups, duets or solos and when it is time for Laura to come on stage I glance at Gerry. He has moved forward in his seat and is rubbing his hands together. I can see he's nervous but is also beaming with pride for his little girl.

The lights come up and Laura is standing in the middle of the stage wearing a white chiffon dress and her feet are bare. To her right is a boy of about the same age, dressed in white jeans and a white shirt. I recognise the music. It's a song called Faded and it's perfect for the type of mid-tempo contemporary dance they are doing. They dance as if they have clouds under their feet and every step tells a story. I am completely spellbound. Laura's dress makes her look like an angel as she dances, and her partner is amazing at holding and lifting her seamlessly. When he throws her in the air and catches her again a huge applause erupts from the audience. She is spun round his neck and at one point he spins on his feet with her held aloft in one hand. As the dance comes to an end, I realise I am crying and I rush to wipe my tears so that no one will notice but it's too late.

"Hey are you okay?" Steven asks.

I shake my head. "That was so beautiful, I... I just got a little carried away by it. She's an amazing young lady isn't she?"

"Oh, she is that. Gerry is so proud of her. She wants to study musical theatre at the Royal Conservatoire of Scotland and Gerry and his ex-wife are doing everything they can to get her there."

"Oh, she'll do it no problem she's so skilled. I'd love to be able to dance, it must feel amazing."

The rest of the show is just as good, and I am left in no doubt that this is a really good dance school. The dancers are all very professional despite their age but more than that they all look like they are having fun on stage. This has been an extremely emotional night for me in one way or another and I am more than ready to go home.

We say our goodbyes to Gerry and Julie, and I congratulate Laura on her dance. As I get into the car, I feel weary and a stuttered sigh rises from my chest. Steven and I look at each other and smile and I feel like the luckiest woman in the world. This man has changed my life in a way I never thought possible and I love him dearly.

CHAPTER 25

"IT'S NICE TO SEE you both together. I'm glad you decided to come along," Nate says leaning back in his chair as Steven and I take a seat on the sofa in front of him.

"Did we really have a choice?" Steven's question is tinged with annoyance, but I know this is only masking the fear he is feeling at having to talk so openly about his father.

"Of course you did, but you already know that. This isn't about choice Steven, it's necessary. Now shall we begin?"

Steven shrugs his shoulders and his demeanour reminds me of a petulant child. Nate looks at us and I know he's waiting for one of us to say something. I take a breath and am about to speak when I see Steven roll his eyes.

"Steven this is ridiculous. Will you get on board here?" I can feel tears threaten to spill. "I don't really want to be here going over all this again. I was terrified for my life, but do you know who I was most worried about? More than anyone else, including my parents and me. It was you," as I start to cry my words come out high-pitched. "I was worried about you and how me being held in that stinking hellhole was hurting you. And then I felt guilty that it was my fault you never got the closure you so deserved with that piece of shit." I put my head in my hands as huge heaving sobs wrack my body.

I feel the sofa move and then I am pulled into Steven's embrace. "I'm so sorry Gina, please forgive me," Steven's breath is hot against my head and I feel my body melt into him. He keeps repeating the word sorry over and over again. I lean back and look at him. His eyes are pleading and glassy with tears.

"It's not about being sorry Steven, it's about accepting what's happened and moving on from it. Can we please talk about this? I'm more than ready to be done with it."

The sound of Nate clearing his throat startles us and we both turn to look at him.

"You're getting too good at self-therapy Gina. But you are right. This isn't about apportioning blame or feeling guilty. What you both need is closure, albeit in different forms." He folds one long leg over the other and readies his notebook and pen. "Let's carry on where you started Gina. I'm going to get right to the point, who do you each think is to blame for what happened to Gina?"

My heart sinks because I know what Steven is going to say.

"Me," Steven says solemnly, not looking at me.

"Colin," I counter and stare at the side of Steven's head, imploring him to look at me, but he doesn't.

"Okay," says Nate. "Now I want you to elaborate and tell me why you have each come to that conclusion.

I can see this is going to be a long session, so I decide to start.

"Colin was the one who started all this, many years before I even knew Steven, before he even existed. This was his doing from the start. He was the one who had an affair; no one made him do it. No one pointed a gun at his head and forced him to pursue a young woman knowing full well that he had made a vow to be faithful to his wife. He is solely to blame for this."

Nate has been writing notes as I have been speaking and now he stops and turns his attention to Steven.

"Mhm, and Steven why do you think you are to blame?"

Steven shakes his head and sighs. "You know

why."

"I know and so does Gina, but you need to say it out loud. Let yourself hear it and I mean really hear it. Listen to what you say and think about it carefully."

Nate is talking to Steven the way I have wanted to for so long. He needs to hear this.

"It's my fault for pursuing Gina. It's my fault that she even came in to contact with him. If she hadn't been with me this would never have happened to her."

Nate adjusts his position in his chair and leans forward. "If it hadn't happened to Gina, who would it have happened to Steven?"

"Probably me but my life isn't worth anything."

My heart is breaking for him. I take his hand and rub his knuckles.

"Tell me why Gina's life is worth more than yours Steven."

"Because she would be missed. I wouldn't. Worthless pieces of shit aren't missed by anyone."

I gasp at how matter of fact he is about how he sees himself and I know those are the words Colin used to describe him. I suppose when you are told the same thing over and over you can actually start to believe it yourself.

"Steven you have a lot of people around you who care for you and love you."

He closes his eyes as he hears my words and a tear

rolls off his cheek. I feel utterly helpless. I don't have a clue what I can do to console him or get him to realise that I'm right. I look at Nate who gives the tiniest shake of his head and I realise what he means instantly. I need to stay quiet and let Steven come to these conclusions himself.

Nate, I have come to understand, has a knack of doing this with people. He has made me see things about myself that, no matter how many people tried to show me, I never wanted to believe.

"Who said you were worthless Steven?" Nate's voice is softer now and more coaxing.

"My dad," he says quietly, almost child-like.

"How did it make you feel when he said those things about you?"

"Sad, unloved I guess."

"And do you really still feel unloved Steven?"

He turns to look at me and gives a small half smile. "Look mate I know what you're saying, and I know it makes sense. I also know you're trying to make me realise it for myself and I do in some way, but I've never felt loved until…" Steven stops and turns his gaze on me. Taking both of my hands in his, he kisses my fingers. "Until I met this perfect human being." He's looking at me but still talking to Nate.

"And how did it make you feel when she was missing?"

"Helpless, sick, desperate. Most of all I felt lonely."

"Can you tell me how many people came to you when Gina was gone?"

"Too many to count. I know they wouldn't have been there if they hadn't cared but I really did feel lonely. Gina is my anchor. She makes me want to live and experience life. I just used to go through the motions of living, but you know this. How often have we talked about it?"

Nate nods in agreement but stays quiet letting Steven continue.

"I was terrified for her because I knew what he was capable of and I also knew that Gina did too. I had told her what he had done. Every time I thought about what was happening to her, I was imagining the terror she must have been feeling." He lets go of my hands and clasps his in front of him. "I'll always blame myself for what happened to her Nate, no matter how much we talk about it or you try to convince me otherwise, we both know if she hadn't known me this wouldn't have happened to her."

"Gina how do you feel about what Steven has said? Do you think he is wrong to blame himself?"

I don't know what to say. Steven is right of course; if I hadn't met him Colin would have had no interest in me.

"He's right," I close my eyes against the rush of

216

tears springing to the fore and as my face wets and I taste the salty water I am consumed by a horrible realisation. "I'm so sorry Steven," I say as my voice cracks and sobs wrack my body.

I pull some tissues from the box on the table in front of me and wipe at my face. Nate and Steven stay quiet until I have calmed down enough continue.

"Gina this is what we needed to get to. Steven knows full well what you mean when you agree with him. I will also say he is right but then so are you. Everything you said about Colin is true and everything Steven has said about himself is true. It's how you both interpret it that's skewed." Nate's voice has an extremely calming effect on me, and I find my composure return quickly.

"I have hated myself every day since that thought first entered my head."

"Gina this was the whole point of today," Nate sits back in his chair again and flips the page in his notebook. "Neither of you have spoken to each other about it. You both know that something like this festering away in the back of your mind can cause all hell to break loose when it rears its ugly head. Most people don't like to admit these feelings to the person they love because they are worried how the other will react or that they will be so hurt by it that there may never be any coming back from it. The problem with not dealing with it head on is that the truth will always come out and most of the time it is during an argument. It could be over something as trivial as who left the toilet seat up or left the freezer door open and spoiled all the food."

Steven and I both smile at this because these are extremely trivial things.

"Yes, Fiona has put my balls in a vice for doing both those things, but I am only using them as examples. You both need to make peace with this and move on from it. Nothing you say or do from now on will change what happened. It has become a part of your past, but you cannot allow it to dictate your future. You won't ever forget it happened but the thoughts of it will get easier to cope with over time."

"Thank you Nate," I say as I tug on Steven's arm and he responds by pulling me in close.

"I'd like to continue to see you both together for another few sessions, but I can tell you that you've made some good progress here today. Remember I'm always here if you need me for anything and try to talk more often and more openly with each other. I promise it will help."

***

"Can I show you something?" I ask Steven as we sit watching TV. Our therapy session with Nate today knocked the stuffing out of us both but it has somehow made me want to share more with Steven and, as Nate said, be more open with him.

"Okay," he replies warily.

"Wait there. I'll be right back."

I run upstairs and grab my camera and my MacBook and bring them back to the TV room. Steven eyes me suspiciously as I sit back down and open up the file on my laptop marked 'BRIDGE'.

"Scroll through these photos and don't say anything until you get to the end," I hand him the laptop and watch as he starts to flick through the photos.

"Why?" Steven asks on a breath when he's finished. I can tell he's trying to stay composed.

"Honestly, I have no idea. Nate told me that it was best not to avoid the bridge. He said it was like getting back in a car after having an accident. The longer you leave it the harder it gets."

"And you didn't feel like you could tell me because you were worried," he sits back and sighs. "I'm so sorry Gina. This shit should have died with that fucker. Come here," he puts the laptop on the table and pulls me into his lap. "I love you Gina and I'll do everything in my power to keep you safe and happy. I have never been more scared in my life than when you were gone. I thought I had lost the only good thing that has ever happened to me."

"Oh Steven," I reach up and caress his cheek. "We'll get through this, I know we will. We're still here, still together and I love you with all my heart. I'm not going anywhere."

"Clean slate then?" He holds his fist up and I bump it with mine.

"Clean slate handsome," I wink at him and he responds by throwing me down on to the couch and looks at me with a renewed passion in his eyes.

Clean slate indeed!

CHAPTER 26

MY EMAIL INBOX HAS been going crazy since I had my meeting with Ed and as I sit at the kitchen table sorting through them all an iMessage flashes up on my screen. It's from Charlie.

Hey babe, I'll be there for around 5 o'clock. Xx

We are '*going out for dinner*'. I know otherwise because I am a bloody nosey, impatient bitch. There's a surprise birthday party happening for me and I really wish I hadn't pried it out of Cerys now.

"Hey gorgeous, what are you up to?"

"Sorting through my emails, there are a million of them." I look up at Steven who has come to stand behind me.

He looks so smart dressed in jeans, white t-shirt and a navy blazer.

"I have something to tell you," he says as he sits at

the seat opposite me.

I hate those words. I always think it's going to be something bad. "Oh."

"No, don't worry, honestly, you're going to love this," he is smiling from ear to ear. "You know the building firm I was meeting with the other day?"

"Yeah." I remember him telling me this was going to be his step into property development.

"Well, I bought an old hotel that morning at an auction and I've secured that building company to convert it."

"A hotel? I thought you were doing houses not hotels. Do you even know how to run a hotel?"

"Well, if you'll let me finish. I was thinking we could convert the building into a residential training facility and run it through Opportunities for Life."

I am completely lost for words. This man never ceases to amaze me. "Wow."

"I'm sorry I didn't run it by you first, this charity is your baby after all."

I put my hand up and stop him. "No, we are in this together. I don't know the first thing about running a charity and also I have no contacts. This is going to be a huge learning curve for me but I'm so excited. And you know what makes it even better? I get to do it with you."

"I think this is going to be one of the best things

I've ever done, next to meeting you. I finally feel like I have a purpose in life now. You know that all my hard work will pay off someday."

I take his hand and smile. "So… Charlie will be here soon. She still hasn't told me where we are going for dinner. Has she said anything to you?"

As much as this man can be as cool as a cucumber when he wants, I notice a tiny twitch on his lips. "I don't know but she did ask for Gerry's services tonight so she's doing it in style. So, thirty-two on Monday eh?" He lets go of my hand and stands up. "You going to start knitting and drinking Horlicks then?" He starts to back away from me.

"Oh, that was below the belt boyo," I get up from my seat and run at him.

He catches me in his arms and kisses me. "I love you Gina. I want to make this the best birthday you've ever had."

"Just being with you is the best birthday ever."

***

Gerry pulls into the entrance of Mar Hall. This is the same place that held the Winter Ball. I know this estate has a huge ballroom in the main building so I assume that's where my party will be.

"This is going to be an expensive dinner Charlie. Are you sure about this?" I try to sound as genuine as

I can as

"No expense spared for my bestie."

I'm caught off guard when Gerry takes a left into a street filled with beautiful mansions. We pull up outside one at the far end and the cul-de-sac is full of recognisable cars. *Nothing like making it obvious guys*, but I don't understand why we are at this house. I look questioningly at Charlie who shrugs her shoulders. She genuinely seems as perplexed as me.

"Just a sec ladies," Gerry pulls down the visor and presses a button on a fob attached to it. The wrought iron gates in front of the car open smoothly without a sound. Gerry waits for them to open then drives the car over the grey mono-block driveway, coming to a stop close to the huge oak and glass front door. I look out the rear windscreen and see the gates close behind us.

"Whose house is this Gerry?" Asks Charlie, and I can tell from her tone that she really has no idea what's going on.

"I don't know, I was just asked to bring you both here."

Charlie looks at me and shrugs. "Well blow me down with a feather, I've been had."

I catch Gerry's reflection in the mirror and see the smile on his face. He knows exactly why we're here. He gets out of the car and opens the door for us. He holds his out arms and we each loop ours through as he leads us up the steps and in through the front door. We enter into a beautiful, spacious vestibule. Through the glass doors ahead of us I can see a stunning hallway and the start of a beautiful oak staircase. The place is dimly lit, just enough for us to not bump into anything.

Gerry leads us through the glass doors and left into what appears to be a living room. As soon as we are through the doors, I get the fright of my life when there is a succession of loud pops and the lights are thrown up full.

"SURPRISE!"

I look round at all the faces. Mum, dad, Mark, Steven and, oh my God, quite a few of my friends from Uni. I haven't seen some of these people in years. There are party popper streamers everywhere and Steven is standing in the middle of the floor with a huge smile on his face. I go to him and throw my arms round his neck.

"Thank you," I whisper as I hug him tight.

"Happy birthday gorgeous."

I let him go and am given hugs and kisses from everyone and am wished happy birthday over and over again. I am completely overwhelmed and so full of love for this thoughtful man.

"Right everyone you can relax now the guest of honour is here," Steven addresses the room as three waitresses appear from nowhere holding trays laden with champagne flutes.

Steven and I take one and he leads me out of the living room and through to another room. A little smaller this time but with a massive semi-circle sofa and a TV the size of a cinema screen on the wall. He closes the door and pulls me to him kissing me softly and slowly. I'm a little breathless when he releases me.

"This is amazing Steven," I whisper

"Oh, this is just the beginning of your birthday weekend. Believe me there is more to come. Sit down, I have something for you," he motions to the couch and I take a seat.

Steven takes my glass and places it on the coffee table in front of the sofa. He takes a small box from a cabinet next to the door and comes to sit next to me. He hands me the box and plants a kiss on my lips.

"Your first present was your surprise party and by the way I know you got Cerys to spill the beans." I feel my cheeks go red. "This is your second present."

My hands are shaking as I open the box. Inside is some black tissue paper and underneath is a set of keys.

"Did you buy me a car?"

"No... I bought you a house."

I think I'm about to have a panic attack. "What?"

Steven waves his hand out in front of him. "This house."

I honestly can't seem to take this in. "What?" I say

226

again shaking my head.

"Tell me I haven't gone too far. I'm starting to wonder if this was such a good idea now," he really sounds worried.

I take his hand. "Steven, this is by far the most wonderful thing anyone has ever done for me. This place is out of this world but why?"

"I want to spend the rest of my life with you Gina and I thought we should do things properly and have our own place together. Remember Andrea Marshall?"

I nod. "Was this her house?"

"Got it in one. When she came to see me and we were going over her plans for selling it I couldn't pass up the opportunity. It was her that gave me the idea of having your party here," he slides off the couch onto his knees in front of me.

"What are you doing Steven?"

"Present three. Gina, I love you with every part of me. You've completely turned my life around and given it meaning beyond anything I could have imagined," he reaches into his blazer pocket and pulls out a small black velvet box.

"Oh my God," I whisper.

"Will you marry me Gina?"

He opens the box and there sits the most beautiful cushion cut diamond surrounded by a row of pink and a row of white diamonds. Inside the lid of the box is a name I know well. Tiffany & Co. I am so glad I'm sitting down right now. I realise I haven't actually said anything yet, but I worry if I try, I might start bawling.

"Are you okay?"

"Yes."

"Yes, you're okay or yes, you'll marry me?"

"Both."

He stands and pulls me up off the couch. His kiss is filled with longing and lust and I'm swept away in the moment.

"Thank you Gina," he whispers against my lips and takes my left hand.

He kisses my ring finger and takes the ring from the box. The cold metal sliding on to my finger makes me shiver and as I hold my hand out in front of me, I can hardly believe what I'm seeing.

"I love you Steven. This is the best birthday ever."

"Can we tell everyone? Not a single soul knows I was planning this, not even Cerys or Gerry."

"You mean you picked this ring yourself?"

He smiles, obviously pleased with himself. "Sure did."

"It couldn't be more perfect Steven thank you. And yes, we can go and tell everyone."

He takes my hand and leads me back to the other side of the house. There are people milling about between the kitchen and the living room and it's noisy with happy chatter. I stop us in the hallway before we reach the living room and take a deep breath.

"You okay?" Steven kisses my hand.

"Yeah. I just need a sec. I'm pretty overwhelmed Steven. You've totally blown me away tonight."

"I know, and I'm afraid I'm not done."

"I don't know if I can take any more surprises tonight."

He nods. "I promise it's only one more. Now let's go, I want to show off my new fiancée."

It sounds so strange but oh so nice.

"Okay, let's do this handsome."

Steven rounds everyone up in the living room and makes sure they all have a drink. When there is quiet, he speaks.

"I would like to start by thanking everyone for making this a very special night for a very special woman," he smiles at me as he addresses the guests. "Gina, you have a heart of gold and I'm so happy that you've given part of it to me. Thank you for agreeing to become my wife. I love you."

He kisses me as a gasp circulates round the room followed by intense chatting and 'oh my God's' and 'congratulations'.

We are swept up in the jubilant atmosphere and everyone examines my hand and they hug me in return. Steven has his hand shaken and his cheek kissed and is almost squashed by my mum who seems unable to let him go. When I see her with him an uneasy feeling falls over me. I remember my parents being this way with Aiden, being so happy for us and welcoming him into our family. I know in my heart that Steven is nothing like him but now that the image is in my head, I'm having a hard time getting rid of it.

CHAPTER 27

THE GUESTS HAVE ALL gone home and the only people left in the house are those staying the night. Everyone is in the kitchen, where all good parties end, and the conversation is extremely loud and drunken. I slip out of the room and sneak upstairs. This is the first time I've been able to see the place and it is magnificent. The bedrooms are all fully furnished, and I wonder if Steven did this or if he bought it like this.

The master bedroom has a beautiful oak four poster bed with no canopy. All the furniture is the same stunning oak as the bed and the full-length glass windows are sure to let loads of light flood in. I take a seat on the bed and look at my engagement ring. It glints under the lights and I feel butterflies in my stomach. This night has been nothing short of crazy and apparently Steven has more to give me. I don't think I've had a birthday like this, apart from the one when I turned ten and got to go to a Spice Girls concert and meet them backstage. I'd say this was the grown-up version of that.

I'm so busy dreaming that I don't immediately notice someone in the room with me.

"Hey sweetheart, are you ok?"

I turn and see my mum standing in the doorway.

"I'm better than fine mum." I hold up my left hand and the diamond and its pink companions glitter and glisten. "Can you believe this?"

"Oh, Gina, I'm so happy for you." She comes to sit beside me on the bed. "You deserve this my darling. After everything you've been through its only fitting that you should get to be truly happy. And I mean truly happy. I know it was sometimes hard work keeping up your front with Aiden."

I frown at her. "What do you mean?"

"Gina, I'm your mother, do you think I didn't see what was happening? I could see you growing apart, but I certainly didn't think it had anything to do with him having an affair."

I look down and shake my head. "He used to pick fights with me all the time. I thought he was just stressed but I realise now he was trying to get me to leave him. Steven is a breath of fresh air compared to that, but I have this amazing ability to always question

232

anything that seems too good to be true, especially now. You don't think we're rushing this do you? We've only been together five months."

"Does it feel right?"

"It really does mum. It's completely different this time. I'm older and wiser and I know he loves me. If I'm honest I think Aiden and I fell into a habit a long time before he died. I just wish he'd told me himself. It feels horrible hating a dead man."

"I only ever want you to be happy and I can see that you are. You've come a long way since you met Steven and I'm so proud of you. Dad thinks the world of him, you know that. He kind of knew about this before you did."

"What?"

"Steven was talking to him and throwing hypothetical questions at him. It wasn't as far as asking his permission or actually telling him outright, but it was obvious enough. He only told me tonight after the fact. You know I hate being kept in the dark, so I'm not impressed with him right now."

I hug her tight. "Oh mum, I love you."

"Carla? Carla, where are you?" My dad's voice booms up the stairs.

"Up here sweetie pie," Mum laughs and flutters her eyelids.

I really hope Steven and I can be like them when

we are older. They've been together for such a long time and still love each other madly. I don't know why I ever doubted him.

Dad appears in the doorway with a whisky in his hand. "Steven has something for us to do before we hit the hay. Are you both coming down?"

"Yeah. This sounds intriguing," I cross the room and give my dad a huge hug. "I love you daddy."

"Aw darling, I love you too and I couldn't be happier for you."

"Let's go and see what that man of yours is up to," mum hooks her arm through mine, and we make our way down stairs.

Everyone is in the TV room and the lights are up full, illuminating the room. In the middle of the floor are two microphones on stands and the TV has a menu page on it. I burst out laughing when I realise Steven's plan. Charlie, Mark, Cerys and Amanda are on the sofa and Steven is fiddling with some cables near the TV. Gerry and Julie are sitting on a very comfy looking chaise.

"Right who's first?" Steven stands and taps the two microphones.

"Meeeee," squeals Cerys.

Amanda rolls her eyes.

"Right, this is the playlist, choose one from the first row," Steven points to the list of songs on a laminated sheet.

"This one," she stabs her finger on the sheet and Steven laughs.

He takes a seat on the stool of the piano that I hadn't noticed was so big earlier. "Are you sure?"

"Fuck yeah," she slaps her hand on her mouth. "I'm so sorry Mr and Mrs Harper."

My dad laughs. "Don't worry my dear, it's fuck all I've not heard or used before."

"Oh my God, Dad!" In my whole life I have rarely heard either of my parents swear. On the odd occasion I did it was when they didn't know I was there. He laughs at me, as my face turns rather red.

The music starts and Cerys has her game face on. It appears she's doing Cher.

I take a seat on Steven's lap and he hugs me tight. "Hi fiancée," he whispers.

"Hi fiancé," I laugh.

Cerys is tapping her foot to the intro and has her eyes closed. She misses the first bar and the whole thing goes to hell as she tries to get it back. She manages to get in time when she reaches the chorus and takes the mic off the stand so that she can move, but we are all laughing so hard that she loses it again. I don't even think she cares. She's doing plenty of moves to go with the words in the song. Her rendition of Gypsies, Tramps and Thieves will go down in history as one of the funniest performances I think I've ever seen. By the time she's done I have tears streaming from my eyes and my stomach hurts.

Poor Cerys. She closes her eyes and bows her head. Amanda glances at me with a helpless look but Cerys is absolutely fine. She keeps her head down, holds out her hand with the mic and drops it. She looks up and says, "We out."

The room erupts in laughter again and Cerys struts her way back to the sofa, fist bumping and high fiving us all as she goes.

Mum and dad are next, and they do a brilliant rendition of Don't Go Breaking My Heart with my dad sitting at the piano pretending to be Elton John. They are so good together and as I watch them and take a moment to appreciate the atmosphere around me, I realise how lucky I am. This is my family, real and found, old and new and I am truly grateful for them all.

***

What should have been a ninety-minute singing session eventually turned out to be almost three hours of complete hilarity. By the time we all get to bed its gone four in the morning.

"Steven, I don't honestly think I have laughed like that in so long thank you so much."

"It was fun wasn't it?" He stands behind me at the

bathroom sink and wraps his arms round me.

I look at us in the mirror. It's a picture of perfection.

"This house is stunning Steven, it truly is and it's huge. You wouldn't know there were five couples staying here tonight. I can't wait to explore it properly."

"Well you'll need to wait to do that, we need to be at the airport for noon."

I eye him suspiciously. "Why?"

"I'll show you." He has that little '*I'm chuffed with myself*' smile on his face as he goes back into the bedroom.

I follow and he hands me a large brown envelope. Sitting down on the bed I open it and pull out a glossy brochure and some other paperwork. The brochure has a picture of a stunning white sandy beach flanked by palm trees and turquoise water. Sapphire Paradise Resort Maldives. Oh my God I think I'm about to pass out, again. I look at Steven, but I can't speak.

"Seven days of total tranquillity, relaxation and us. Happy birthday Gina."

"Steven," my voice is a whisper. I open the brochure and flick through the pages, each one more beautiful than the last. "I don't... thank you."

"I told you I'd give you the moon if I could Gina. I love you and I want you to be happy."

I shake my head and take his hand. "Just being with

you makes me happy you know that. I don't need anything else, but oh man am I looking forward to this. You know I would have been happy with a card and some flowers."

He laughs. "Well I thought you could do with a fiancé, a house and a holiday."

"Yeah about the house. Why? I love your place."

"Oh, we're keeping that one too. A city crash pad if you like. This house is an investment for the future. Our future."

"I love you Steven Parker," I kiss him and my heart is full to bursting. My future looks as bright as the sun, I just hope it doesn't fizzle out.

CHAPTER 28

MY FLOWING WHITE SUNDRESS wafts gently in a warm breeze as I stand on the arrival pavilion of the Maldivian resort where we will be spending the next seven days. The seaplane ride gave us some stunning views of the most beautiful chain of islands I've ever seen. I feel as though I have stepped into a dream. What better way to celebrate our engagement than to do it in paradise?

"Mr Parker, Ms Harper welcome to Sapphire Paradise Resort. My name is Tahlia. Champagne?"

Tahlia is carrying a silver tray with two champagne flutes filled with golden, bubbling heaven. She is perfectly turned out and has an accent I can't place.

We each take a glass and Steven holds his up to me. "Cheers gorgeous."

I clink my glass on his. "Cheers handsome."

"May I take this opportunity to say on behalf of all of us here congratulations on your engagement?" Tahlia says with one of those whiter than white-toothed smiles.

"Umm thank you." I look at Steven who shrugs and smiles.

"If you'll both follow me, Sonny here will take you to the reception area to get booked in before you transfer to your villa by speedboat. Nice and private."

"Sir, madam," Sonny directs us to what looks like a golf cart.

We get in and I take a long drink of my champagne, taking in the azure blue water and clear sky for as far as the eye can see. Sonny turns the cart and we trundle along the jetty.

The reception area is a stunning wooden structure with a thatched roof similar to the arrival pavilion. Everything is so streamlined and minimalistic, but it still makes an impact. The music playing is Zen-like and every staff member we talk to is pleasant and sincere. They also all seem to know our names.

"Mr Parker, Ms Harper," the man at the reception desk nods his head to us. "Welcome to Sapphire. My name is Hassan," he points to his badge. "We are very pleased to meet you and look forward to serving your every need."

I look at Steven and can't help smiling. This is

luxury at its best.

"Okay so you are in our Water Villa. Your butler for your stay is Andy and he will be travelling with you this morning."

A butler, holy hell this *is* luxury. I think this smile might be permanently stuck on my face for the week at this rate. Hassan checks us in and takes our glasses, then we are driven back to the jetty by Sonny. There is a white speedboat waiting at the dock and Tahlia is standing beside a tall, fair-haired man. As we come to a stop, they both come to greet us.

"Hello again. This is your butler Andy, he will be travelling with you to the Villa."

Andy nods to us. "Mr Parker, Ms Harper pleased to meet you," he greets us with an American accent and shakes both of our hands.

We board the boat and are taken the short distance to our villa. As we come to a stop at the jetty of the most beautiful villa I've ever seen, Steven squeezes my hand. "You okay?"

"I am. This is out of this world Steven; I honestly can't believe this is real."

"It is spectacular. This is somewhere I've always wanted to visit but I never had the right person to go with."

I reach up and stroke his cheek. "I love you Steven, thank you. I couldn't think of anyone else I'd rather share this journey with, and I don't just mean being here. I mean the rest of my life."

"Okay guys, let's get you settled in." Andy makes his way from the boat and onto the jetty then stands at the foot of the steps leading up to the wooden walkway.

Steven gets out before me and helps me out. As I ascend the stairs the villa comes into full view. I gasp.

"Oh my God this is beautiful," I look back at Steven who is smiling.

"Your luggage is waiting in your bedroom for you and I have prepared a light dinner for you both," Andy leads us through a set of doors and into a dining area. "Would you like to eat here or out at the dining gazebo?" He motions to the spread of food on the table.

"I think we'll eat here. We can do tonight's dinner out there," says Steven.

"Very good sir," Andy pulls out a chair for me and does the same for Steven. "I will be in my quarters just over there if you need me," he points to a small chalet in the water around a hundred yards away from our villa. "Please feel free to call on me for anything you need at any time."

"Thank you Andy," we both say at the same time and watch him disappear back lout the way we came in.

"Steven this food looks amazing."

"It does. Is there a menu so we know what we're eating?"

I look around the table and notice a piece of ivory card sticking out from under a silver tray of champagne and water.

"This'll be it." I pull it out and read the gold embossed writing.

Dear Mr Parker and Ms Harper,

Thank you for joining us at Sapphire Paradise Resort. We hope you enjoy your stay with us and have the most relaxing holiday. Please be assured we will do our utmost to make your stay with us a memorable one.

Our warmest welcome
From all the staff at
Sapphire Paradise Resort

Well this is what I call luxury. "This place is amazing. Not just the look of the place but the attention to detail is absolutely on the ball."

Steven reaches across the table and takes my hand, rubbing my engagement ring. "Only the best for my beautiful girl. Happy birthday, for real this time," he kisses my knuckles. "Now what are we eating?"

As we feast on seared scallops, oysters and shrimp cocktail I let my cares melt away. I'm going to enjoy this little slice of heaven with this angel of a man by my side.

CHAPTER 29

"STAND BETWEEN THE TREES," I shout to Steven.

He walks to the spot I'm pointing at. "Here?"

"Yeah, now hold your hands up."

We are trying to do one of those daft photos everyone does. Those shots where someone is holding the moon in their hand or pushing the Leaning Tower of Pisa back upright. Steven holds his hands up so that it looks like he's pushing the trees apart. He makes a face as if he's straining to push them and I take the shot before I die from laughing. He runs towards me and I show him the photo on the screen of the camera.

"Christ, I look constipated."

"Yeah I think we'll keep that one to look at if we ever need a laugh."

Steven laughs. "Always happy to help. What do

you want to do today?"

"I really don't know but I do know I can't leave this place without at least getting some nice shots. This is a photographer's dream."

"I know where you could take some amazing pictures."

"Where?"

"Underwater."

"Ehm no."

"Why not, are you scared of the water?"

"No, my camera isn't waterproof. I don't even have an underwater housing for it."

"Ah well, there happens to be a fantastic water sports base here so I'm sure they'll have something to fit your camera."

"That sounds like a plan then. I read in the brochure this morning that there's a reef here so maybe I can get some shots of the cute little fishes."

"Yeah and the sharks," Steven takes my hand leading us off the beach and towards the main buildings.

***

I was pleasantly surprised by the amount of different sized waterproof camera housings the water sports place had and we found one that fit mine perfectly. The instructor is taking us out to the edge of the island so that we can go snorkelling. I'm just not comfortable with scuba diving at the reef and we'd need more instruction for that.

We were given an hour of instruction in the pool on how to use the breathing apparatus, how to do duck dives and swim with fins on our feet. They also showed us how to signal for help if we get into difficulty. To say I'm apprehensive is an understatement. I really do prefer dry land, but this is such a stunningly unspoilt place that we would be mad not to see it and Steven seems so excited. The water is lovely and warm. The sand and water here are similar to the Hebrides, but the striking difference is about twenty-five degrees. We wade further into the water and the instructor gives us the go ahead.

Steven nods to me. "Ready?"

"No," I smile awkwardly.

We are still on our feet, so I don't even know why I'm so worried.

"You'll be fine. Camera ready?"

"Mhm."

"Let's go then."

We kick off from the bottom and glide through the clear water. After breathing in a little water on my first duck dive, I soon get the hang of it and we swim with the current until we are far enough out to start seeing some marine life. I snap pictures of some of the most beautifully coloured little creatures I've ever seen. I get one of Steven pretending to kiss a yellow fish and another one as he scares it away because he tried to touch it. I catch a turtle, some eels and a small, very cute black tip shark. I never thought I'd put shark and cute in the same sentence, but I suppose there's a first for everything.

***

Our forty minutes in the water flew by so quickly I was actually a little sad to have to leave. Now, as we lounge on a private cabana soaking up the sun, I feel relaxed and content. I don't know where Steven got the sunscreen he's applying to my back, but it smells divine. It's so fruity it's making my mouth water. He unties the back strings of my bikini.

"Hey, you're lucky no-one can see us, you can't do that here."

"As long as you don't turn onto your back, you'll be fine. Anyway, this part of the beach is so quiet, I doubt anyone would notice."

I bat my hand behind me, but he moves and I miss, smacking myself instead.

"Ooh, spanking yourself now. I must not be pleasing you enough."

"Believe me, you please me every day."

He runs his hands up my back and slides them

under me, cupping my breasts.

"Steven," I whisper.

"Shh, there's nobody here," he gives my nipples a tweak and then his hands are gone.

I make a little moan in protest and crane my neck to look at him. He's sitting with his back against the cabana and has picked up his iPad. He looks at me and winks and I sigh. Defeated I put my head down and all of a sudden feel rather sleepy. Our few hours in the water have exhausted me. Closing my eyes, I allow the warmth of the sun to carry me away to sleep and dream for a while.

CHAPTER 30

"GINA, ARE YOU OKAY?" Steven sounds panicked standing outside the bathroom door.

I can't speak for fear that I might start retching again. I have already lost all of my beautiful dinner to the porcelain God and I know there can't be anything left in my stomach.

"Gina please, open the door, I'm worried."

I'm not worried. I know exactly what is going on here. The last few days have had me wondering if there is a possibility I could be pregnant after all. I have resisted the temptation to do a test because we've been having such a lovely time, I didn't want to interrupt it.

"I'm fine Steven. Can you make me cup of tea with no milk? I think it might help."

"Of course as long as you're okay."

"I am thank you."

When I know he is away from the door, I grab my toiletry bag from beside the sink and find the spare pregnancy test I got the day Charlie went into labour. I'm glad I've still got it; there isn't exactly a local chemist here. I open it and proceed to pee on the stick. Here we go again. This time I'm not terrified. I'm not trying to close the hole in the pit of my stomach. This time I am happy. I know how Steven feels about having children now and I have to admit I am rather excited to see the result.

I have mentally counted that my four minutes are up, and I steady my breathing as I turn the test over. The appearance of two very dark pink lines makes me smile so wide I fear it may split my face in two. I put it in my skirt pocket and make my way to the dining area. The sun is setting and it's casting a calming orange glow over the villa. I find Steven sitting at the table with two mugs of tea in front of him. As soon as he sees me, he stands up and pulls me into his warm body.

"Are you okay? I hope you haven't got food poisoning."

I smile and push myself back from him. "No, they haven't poisoned me. Close your eyes."

"What's going on?"

"Will you just do as you are told?"

He eyes me suspiciously and I try as hard as I can

251

not to give anything away. "Okay, okay," He smiles as he closes his eyes.

"Hold out your hands." I place the stick on his upturned palms and stand back slightly as he opens his eyes.

He looks right at me, not at his hands. He knows exactly what it is, but he doesn't take his eyes from mine. Very slowly a smile forms on his lips and his eyes crinkle at the corners as his smile gets bigger and brighter. We stand smiling at each other for a few silent moments before Steven finally moves. He puts the test down on the table and sweeps me off my feet holding me tight. He still hasn't looked at it.

"Gina, thank you."

I giggle as he puts me back on my feet. "For what?"

"For making my life finally mean something."

Tears spring to my eyes and so begins the pregnancy mood swings of the biggest emotional wreck on the planet.

***

The clinic at the resort is small but very well equipped. I didn't even know there was a clinic here.

"Will you sit down Steven? You're making me nervous."

"I can't," he comes over to the bed and puts his hands on either side of me. "I'm so happy Gina, I can't even tell you."

I reach up and cup his face. "You are going to be the best dad in the world Steven."

"I hope you're right."

"Steven, I'm a female, I'm always right."

He laughs as Shanna, the nurse we met on arrival at the clinic, enters the room.

"Ms Harper, Mr Parker how are you both?"

"I'm fine but this one is a little nervous."

"Oh, you're not the first father-to-be I've met who's nervous. Now let's get you checked over. Of course, I advise you to go straight to your doctor and get your pre-natal care set up when you get home."

"Yes, I will."

"Okay, so I did a dip test and you are definitely pregnant. Congratulations both of you."

We both smile at each other. I'm going to have sore cheeks by the time this day is over.

"I'll check your blood pressure and give you some multi-vitamins to start taking. And if you have any problems while you're here come straight over. Even if it's only to get some advice, I'm here for the rest of this week."

"Thank you so much Shanna." I stop talking as she takes my blood pressure.

"You're good Gina, nice healthy blood pressure. All you need to do is get plenty of rest and that shouldn't be an issue here. It is paradise after all."

***

The daybed at the villa is on its own deck off a walkway from the main house and is the perfect place to watch the sunset. We have been out here since late afternoon and Steven hasn't let me go since we came back from the clinic, and I haven't wanted him to.

"I can't believe this Gina," Steven runs his hand over my belly. "How far along do you think you are?"

"I honestly don't know, seven or eight weeks, but I have a feeling that when I tested before it was a false negative or maybe the line just wasn't clear enough. When I took that test, I hadn't taken my pill for two weeks. I kind of forgot about it after the... well you know. The last one I had taken was that day, but you knew that anyway. I just thought my body was adjusting to being off the pill and that's why I haven't had a period. Or the stress of everything that's happened to us over that last few months."

"It really has been stressful. That's why I brought us here. I think we needed this. And I can't think of anywhere more perfect than here to find out we are going to be parents," he smiles. "God Gina I'm going to be a dad. If someone had told me six months ago all this was going to happen to me, I'd have laughed and told them to fuck off."

"Hey, you're not the only one. Christ I was widowed less than a year ago. To anyone looking in on this and knowing nothing about us I must look like a terrible person but believe me when I tell you I am happier than I have ever been in my entire life and it's because of you."

He reaches up and strokes my cheek. "I love you Gina, you and this little one here are the best things that have ever happened to me. Thank you," he kisses me softly.

I lift my leg over his and turn onto my side, getting as close as I can to him. We kiss for a long time, the tension building in the air as the sun starts to set in front of us. The deck out here is completely obscured from anywhere else on the island. Steven pulls the bow behind my neck allowing my bikini to loosen and fall down exposing one of my breasts. He takes it in his hand.

"Do they hurt?" He whispers.

"No. Not yet."

"Good," he closes his mouth over my nipple and flicks it with his tongue. Sparks shoot right to my groin and my hips buck involuntarily.

"Bite it," I surprise myself with that; dirty talk has never been my thing.

"With pleasure," he discards my bikini top then does what I told him and bites my nipple, not too hard but enough to make me moan. He pushes me on to my back and moves to the other nipple. He bites this one a little harder and I can't help myself.

I pull the strings loose on the sides of my bikini bottoms and touch myself. I'm so turned on that I'm already wet. Steven puts his hand over mine and presses ever so slightly. It doesn't take much before I come and it obviously makes Steven more aroused as he shimmies out of his shorts and rises up over me, his erection hard and hot.

"I'll take it slow and gentle," he whispers.

"No," my protest makes his brow furrow.

"I don't want to hurt you."

"You won't, now stop talking and just fuck me will you."

He laughs as he pushes himself inside me, slower than I would like but as soon as he's there he really goes for it. He grabs my hands and pushes them above my head, linking our fingers together as his thrusts become rhythmic and my hips move to meet each one.

There is only the sound of the water lapping beneath us and our ragged breaths and groans as we climax one after the other. As I look into the beautiful blue eyes of the man I love, I know, no matter where we are in the world, this is home. He is home.

CHAPTER 31

OUR SUITCASES ARE PACKED and I'm feeling a little down. I really don't want to leave; this island now holds a special place in my heart. My yellow chiffon dress is swaying in the breeze wafting through the villa. I smooth it down and catch my reflection in the full-length mirror in the bedroom. I don't know if I'm seeing things but I'm sure there is a little bump there. As I'm standing side on running my hands over my belly, I almost have a heart attack when Steven appears in the room from nowhere.

"Jesus Steven. Don't creep up on me like that."

"Sorry babe." He stands behind me and places both hands on my belly. "How's my little bean doing?"

I laugh at him.

"I honestly don't even know it's there. If I'm honest, I'm a little disappointed I haven't had any symptoms yet. Well except the vomiting the other night. There hasn't really been anything glaringly obvious."

"Do you really want sore tits and spewing every minute of the day? Not to mention the…"

I cut him off. "Do not even mention that which should not be mentioned. I already got the run down on *that* from Charlie." The last thing I want to think about right now is not being able to sit down properly for the rest of my pregnancy.

"Okay, I won't mention the haemorrhoids," he laughs and bolts through the wide-open doors, out onto the deck.

I give chase and I think he's going to stop there but, in true Steven fashion, he goes that bit further running across the sand of the little beach and jumping straight into the water.

"Oh my God Steven, we need to leave soon. What are you doing?"

He jumps up from the water punching the air. "I'm going to be a daddy."

I can't help but laugh at him. He's usually so controlled and I must admit it's nice to see him lose it a little.

"Get out of there you nutter."

He climbs out of the water, his wet feet getting covered in sand and walks back towards me. He stops on the deck, dripping wet. I see a sparkle in his eyes, and I know what's behind it. I turn and run as fast as I can, but I don't get far before he's up behind me. He lifts me in his arms and I feel the water soaking through my dress as he carries me into the bedroom.

"You're getting me wet."

"I hope so," he places me on the bed and strips naked. His body is beautifully tanned and glows in the afternoon sun. "Sit up."

I do and he peels the wet dress over my head, discarding it on the floor. He takes off my underwear and lies on the bed beside me.

"We have two hours before we need to check out and I want to make slow, sweet love to my fiancée in paradise one last time."

***

Glasgow is decidedly soggier than the Maldives and I feel the chill in the air as we exit the airport. Steven and I both have a lovely glow on our skin and I am positively beaming inside. I can't believe everything that has happened in the last week. In fact, my life has been one drama after another since I met Steven and I very much doubt most relationships would have survived it.

I stop Steven before we get to the car park. "Let's not tell anyone about the baby until we've had it confirmed here." I motion to Gerry who is a bit in front of us pushing the trolley full of our luggage. I know Steven looks up to Gerry as a sort of father figure and I know he'll be over the moon for us both.

"Not a problem. We can get that organised first thing in the morning," he kisses the top of my head and we catch up with Gerry.

"So you two, did you have a nice holiday?"

"Oh Gerry, it was wonderful. I didn't want to come home, but we missed you too much," I shove his shoulder.

"Aw, I know I'm irresistible," he laughs as he loads the luggage into the Range Rover.

"No Bentley today Gerry?"

Gerry's face turns a little pale. "Ehm about that," he turns to Steven. "There was a little incident while you were gone. Nothing major but I didn't want to interrupt your holiday."

My happy post-holiday mood crashes around me and, while Gerry seems positive that it was nothing, I am sure this is going to be yet another drama to add to my collection.

"Spill," Steven doesn't sound angry, but his tone is clipped.

We all get into the car and Gerry turns to face us in the back seat. "Well... eh... Cerys..."

Steven laughs. "How did I know this was going to

have something to do with Cerys? I swear I sometimes wonder if that girl actually has any brain cells in that beautiful head of hers. What did she do?"

"I was dropping her at home after work on Friday. She was very animated because she managed to set up some meeting you were on about before you left." Steven nods and smiles. This is obviously good news to him. "Well when she went to get out of the car, she sat up too quickly and too far forward and banged right into the rear-view mirror. That tiny hit sent a huge crack right through the windscreen."

"Oh, you beauty! I love having something to tease her about. It's so easy and this is perfect."

I shake my head at him. "Will you leave that poor girl alone? You're so mean to her."

"She just about shit herself. Poor lassie was in tears worried about what you would say."

"Well thankfully that's all it was, I thought you were going to say you'd crashed it, or it had been stolen. Did you get my message the other day?"

"I did. I took delivery yesterday morning."

"Excellent. Did you have it stored where I specified?"

"Sure did."

I look between the two of them and wonder what that was about. When Steven smiles at me I know the look by now. He has something up his sleeve and knowing him it won't be something small either. This man doesn't do small.

CHAPTER 32

SINCE I AM STILL registered with my doctor at the practice where I used to live, Steven has taken me to the private surgery he uses, and I have registered there. The reception staff are lovely and welcoming and the whole atmosphere of the surgery is relaxed and informal. We spent about five minutes filling out forms and only had to wait a few minutes before we were called.

Dr Kelly is a young, very tall brunette woman with the most beautiful, soft, Irish accent.

"Okay my love if you just want to get yourself up on the bed we'll get started."

She pulls a trolley filled with lots of implements and what looks like a walkie-talkie with a microphone attached to it next to the bedside.

"Right Gina, if you can just lie back and unbutton

your trousers, we'll try and get a heartbeat for you."

I do as she asks and Steven takes my hand. Dr Kelly puts a squirt of gel onto the little microphone thing and presses it onto my lower abdomen. It's cool but not uncomfortably cold. She fiddles with a little dial and a static sound comes through the speaker. As she moves it around it makes strange little pops and squeaks. She stops when she gets the right place and I hear the most beautiful sound in the world; my baby's heartbeat.

"Oh, that's a good heartbeat Gina. You're cooking up a wee smasher in there."

I look at Steven who has tears in his eyes. That sets me off and in no time we are a blubbering mess. Before long both of us are in hysterics and I fear Dr Kelly is going to have us committed.

"Sorry doctor. We are just so happy. I promise we will behave from now on."

She puts her hand on my shoulder. "Don't apologise Gina you're well within your rights to be happy. Congratulations to you both."

She wipes off the instrument and my belly and returns the trolley. "Now let's try and get you a due date. Do you know when your last period was?"

"Ehm no. I was on the pill, but I had forgotten to take it so…"

"Okay how many had you missed?"

"About fourteen."

Dr Kelly's eyes almost pop out of her head, but she smiles. "Gosh I've heard of people missing one or two but fourteen. Holy moly you didn't do this by half."

I know she doesn't know what happened to me, but I feel a little stupid right now. Unfortunately, I am finding it really hard not to cry at the drop of a hat these days and that's exactly what I do.

"Oh Gina, I am so sorry I didn't mean to upset you."

Steven reassures her. "It's okay. There was an incident at the start of the year that we'd rather forget about and that's why she missed her pills."

"Understood. I'm sorry, let's start that again. So, when did you take your last pill?"

"Fourteenth of January." I dry my eyes with the tissue Dr Kelly gave me.

"And have you been using another form of contraceptive since you realised.?"

"Yes, we have."

She fiddles with a round chart and makes a note in my file. "Okay I get a due date of around the twenty ninth of October which means you are around nine weeks pregnant." She smiles at us. "It's a little early for a scan but I'll do one, we should be able to see something."

"Really, you'll be able to see it?"

"Oh yes, we should get a decent picture of the baby

and we can try to get a more accurate date for you."

"Oh yes please."

"Now do you have any questions for me?"

"I do actually," I look at Steven and he frowns. "Um…I've been drinking alcohol all through this, not to excess but I'm a little worried I might have harmed the baby."

"Honestly Gina, if you've not gotten yourself blind drunk and it's only been one or two at a time, I wouldn't beat myself up about it. Obviously, I will advise against it from now on though," she nods her head reassuringly.

"Thanks so much, you've really put my mind at ease."

Dr Kelly wheels an ultrasound machine next to the bed. She puts some more gel on my belly and runs her little implement over it. She presses down and I watch the screen. She presses some buttons and the image on the screen stills.

"So guys, there's your wee baby," she points out the head, the body and the heartbeat.

Steven and I look on in awe. I can't believe there is the beginning of a tiny human, our tiny human, in my belly.

***

I run my thumb over the set of scan pictures on my

knee. I'm still rather shocked by the turn of events and my mind is all over the place.

"Are you okay?" Steven interrupts my thoughts.

I nod. "I'm fine. This has been a wild ride hasn't."

"You're not kidding. I still can't believe we're going to be parents Gina. I mean me, a dad. It's crazy," he shakes his head and looks out the window of the car.

I put my hand on his. "Steven, you are going to be the best dad in the world, trust me."

"Thank you. It means a lot to have someone believe in me."

"Plenty of people believe in you. Your problem is more self-doubt than anything else."

Steven laughs. "Christ, you could give Nate a run for his money you know."

"I try. God help us when he finds out about this," I squeeze his hand. "Right let's go and figure out how to tell everyone this amazing news. And we need to do it in Steven style. You know that '*spring it on you and knock you on your arse*' type of announcement."

He laughs. "Well, what good would this world be without Steven style surprises?"

CHAPTER 33

"OH MY GOD, OH my God, oh my God."

I think my mum is about to have a panic attack. She and dad have just looked closer at the photo Steven has taken. It took mum a few seconds to realise what we had done but now she's hysterical.

I had sat on the sofa between them and opened up my cardigan revealing a t-shirt that said, *'WE'RE HAVING A BABY'*.

"Are you happy mum?"

She gets up and drags me off the couch into a tight hug. "Oh my baby is having a baby. Come here you," she pulls Steven into the hug too. "I'm so happy for you both."

Dad is still sitting on the couch in silence staring at the phone.

"Daddy are you okay?"

"Oh Gina, you have no idea," he takes my hand.

I sit beside him. "I do dad, I really do. I couldn't be happier."

"I'm so proud of you both. I love you my beautiful girl," he hugs me tight.

"I love you too daddy."

For the next hour we all sit chatting and mum takes great pleasure in giving me a rundown of the whole nine months of her pregnancy with me. And as ever there is no stone left unturned. I leave their house with a definite plan to have all the drugs I can get my hands on.

"We need to go to the new house."

I eye Steven suspiciously as we leave my parent's driveway. "Why?"

"There's something I need to show you."

"What is it?"

"It's a surprise."

"Oh for goodness sake Steven you need to quit this with the surprises. You know I hate them."

He laughs. "I know that's why I like doing it."

"You're so bad." I swat his arm.

We drive to the house in comfortable silence listening to music, both of us singing along now and then. As we approach the gates Steven presses the button on his fob and they open. He drives up to the double garage doors and presses another button and the garage door opens. Inside sits a beautiful, gunmetal grey convertible Range Rover. The registration plate reads 61NA. *Gina*. I look from the car to Steven and back to the car.

"Are you kidding me right now? When the hell did you do this?"

"I ordered it the night you drove this. I saw how much fun you had driving again and this is one hell of a cool car. Of course, had I known you were pregnant I might have got the non-convertible version."

I'm overwhelmed. "It's lovely Steven but seriously how much money have you spent on me over the last few weeks?"

"What does it matter? It's only money and there's plenty of it."

"How much are you worth exactly? I'm not being nosey but…" I look at my engagement ring and twist it round my finger. "…well I am going to be your wife and we are having a baby together so…"

He cuts me off.

"At the moment around two hundred and fifty million pounds."

"Shit," my voice is a whisper.

"Like I said its only money. It meant nothing to me until I found you. I didn't really do anything except work. I made most of my money designing a few buildings in New York and parts of Europe, but it was never really about the money you know. I just enjoyed the thrill of seeing my work being built."

I can't think of anything to say. When I found out he was a millionaire I was expecting it to be about two or three million. Never did I expect it to be as much as much as hundreds of millions.

"Gina are you okay?"

I realise I've been quiet for too long. "I'm fine I'm just a little shocked. That's a lot of money."

"Yeah it is but it doesn't define me. I'd be the same person with or without the money. There's that saying '*Money can't buy happiness*' and it's true it can't. I made my money fast and I'm still young enough to enjoy it, but it never made me happy. Then I met you and the money gave me the means to make you happy."

"Steven you don't need to buy me or my happiness. I love you, and just being with you makes me happier than I've ever been. More so now that we have this wee one on the way."

"I'm not trying to buy you Gina. I'd give it all up now if it were a choice between you or the money. Being able to put some of it to good use in our charity makes me realise that I could have done this kind of thing a long time ago. It took someone with fresh eyes and a different outlook on life to make me see it."

I take his hand.

"I understand, but honestly all I need is you, the money is irrelevant."

"Gina you do realise that when we are married the money will be yours too? Now do you want to drive your new car, or will we leave it to another day?"

"Let's leave it today and come back over when I can get my head round all this."

"Okay," Steven closes the garage door.

"And Steven."

"Yes."

"Please, no more surprises okay?"

"I promise," he gives me a wink and I know my plea has fallen on deaf ears.

***

Since we have told my parents about the baby it's time to tell all of our friends. We are doing it in the guise of a mini engagement party at the apartment. Charlie and Mark are coming in from Edinburgh and Gerry and Julie are picking up Cerys and Amanda.

"Gina how many people are coming tonight again?" Steven surveys the feast in front of him.

"Well people might be hungry. I know I am." I pop a hot mini quiche into my mouth and instantly regret it as it burns the roof of my mouth. "Oh thittt."

"Spit it out for God sake woman."

I hold up my hand and suck in some air to try and

cool the food quickly. I swallow it when it's safe. "Never come between a pregnant woman and her food."

Steven lifts me off my feet and sits me down on a bar stool. "This might sound very clichéd, but you are positively glowing."

"I'll tell you I actually feel great. I'm so excited to tell everyone. Charlie is going to freak out."

"Yeah I'm thinking ear plugs might have been a good addition to tonight."

I slap his arm. "Hey that's my best friend you're talking about."

"I know and I love her to bits."

"Right, they'll be here soon so is the tray ready?"

He winks at me. "Sure is. I just hope they all want a drink."

"Oh they will."

The intercom buzzer sends a shiver of excitement down my spine.

"Showtime babe." Steven leaves me and goes to answer the door.

I get down from the stool and smooth out my dress. I definitely have a tiny bump, but I doubt anyone would notice if they weren't in the know. I hear a commotion in the hallway and our friends make their way into the kitchen.

"Hi everyone," I greet them all hugging everyone

in turn.

Steven picks up the tray full of champagne flutes. "Champagne folks?"

Everyone takes a glass and stands ready for a toast. Steven flips the tray round and holds it in front of him. We have put a sign on the tray saying, '*We're having a baby*.' I watch as the realisation hits their faces one by one.

Charlie is the first to say something. "Oh, shit no way. Are you serious?"

I nod. "Yep."

"Ahhhhhh," she screams and runs at me and I look at Steven.

"I told you, ear plugs," he laughs as Gerry gives him a huge hug.

I see genuine tears of joy in the man's eyes and he is patting Steven's back with so much emotion. "I'm so proud of you son, you're going to be a brilliant dad."

Everyone is so happy for us and the night is filled with love and laughter. We eat and drink the night away, no alcohol for me of course, and it's lovely to know that we have such a great support network. Charlie is going to guide me through this pregnancy in her own special way and I'm pretty sure by the time I'm ready to have this baby I'm probably going to want to be knocked out. Gerry is going to have car seats fitted to all the cars and Cerys has offered for her and

Amanda to decorate a room here as a nursery. If that goes well, and they don't kill each other, they'll do another one at the new house for us too.

We are all sitting in the living room and as I watch everyone chatting and laughing, I know I'm truly happy. No matter what has gone on before this, Steven and I have found our happy ending.

EPILOGUE

MY IVORY WEDDING DRESS is embroidered down one side with sequins and Swarovski crystal diamantes'. The sunlight flooding in through the floor to ceiling windows of my bedroom in the new house glints off them and reflects onto the walls. I feel like a disco ball. Turning to the side and looking at my profile in the full-length mirror I realise I probably *look* like a disco ball. My dress has had to be altered at least four times in the last three months to accommodate my changing shape. There is a knock at the door and Charlie shouts through to me.

"Hey honey do you need a hand with anything, the cars will be here soon?"

"Yes please," I shout back.

She walks into the room in her beautiful pale pink 50's inspired bridesmaid dress. She is carrying a sleeping baby Georgie in her arms who is dressed in a miniature version of her mummy's dress.

"Can you loosen these ribbons for me? I'm getting squished here."

"Babe I really feel for you, but it is going to be so much fun watching you get fat."

"Okay I deserve that, now hurry up before I pass out."

She lays Georgie in the middle of my huge bed. "I still can't believe you're going to be a mummy Gina," says Charlie as she starts loosening the back of my dress.

The relief is instant and I place my hands on my belly. "Neither can I, believe me."

"Right. How's that?"

"Much better, thanks honey. I think my mum thought she was lacing up a corset when she did it earlier."

Charlie pulls me in to a hug. "Okay I'm off to find my errant sister. I have a feeling she'll be propping up the bar later at the reception. I don't know what's wrong with her right now. She must be out of sorts after the move and the new job. She's doing my head in today." She kisses my cheek. "Love you honey, see you soon." She lifts Georgie before heading out the door in a haze of pink chiffon.

Sitting down on the bed, I take stock of the crazy

turn my life has taken over the last seven months.

"Well little one this has been a wild ride hasn't it?" I say to my bump. My engagement ring glistens in the sunlight, mingling with the sparkles of my dress and my mind begins to wander, thinking over all the craziness that brought me here. My daydream comes to an abrupt halt as I get the strange sensation of being on a rollercoaster and my belly takes a nosedive.

"Oh my God!" I say out loud.

I sit still with my hand on my belly, not sure I felt what I think I did. It goes again.

"Well hello little one. What a day to put an appearance in eh?"

I am a little startled when the door opens and my dad peeks his head round.

"Hey sweetheart are you ready to go? The cars are here and I think your chief bridesmaid is about to have a breakdown."

I give a little laugh at the thought of Charlie bossing everyone around. "Yes dad I'm ready as I'll ever be."

My dad walks in, looking so handsome in his kilt. He stands in front of me and holds both of my hands in his.

"My beautiful girl I am so proud of you. Your mum and I are so happy for you both. Steven is a wonderful young man and I know you'll be very happy together. This little one is so lucky." He puts his hand on my bump and looks at me with teary eyes.

"Oh daddy please don't set me off I don't have time to sort my make-up."

We both laugh as we head out the door.

***

Steven and I are being married in the Hunter Halls of Glasgow University, and as I stand outside the large doors with my dad at my side, I feel so happy it's overwhelming. I look back at Charlie standing behind me and instantly wish I hadn't. She is bawling her eyes out. I feel tears well up and I shake my head. No! I mustn't cry now because I know when I get through these doors and see my husband-to-be I am going to be a wreck.

As the doors are opened, my very special entrance music starts. I take a steadying breath and nod to my dad. We walk down the aisle to '*Nuvole Bianche*', the first music Steven and I ever listened to together. I can see the man himself at the end of the aisle, but he keeps his back to me until we are around twenty feet away. When he turns to me, his smile could light up the whole world and right now, in this moment, I don't think I could be happier. As soon as my dad has left my side and I am standing beside Steven nothing else matters. He leans in to me and whispers in my ear.

"You are stunning my angel."

We are married in front of all our loved ones and as we walk out of the hall as husband and wife, I now get the saying *'everything happens for a reason'*. Everything that has happened until now was supposed to happen to get us to this point. I am reminded of something Steven said the day I met him. *'Do you believe in meant to be?'* I didn't then but I do now. I know with all my heart and soul that this is meant to be.

The End.

Thank you so much for taking the time to read Gina and Steven's story. Don't worry, you haven't heard the last of them.

Keep up to date with news of upcoming releases by visiting:

www.clstewart.co.uk

Sign up for exclusive content and offers.

SHATTERED SOUL

"Why did he have to die? Why couldn't he have just left me? Then I could hate him and not feel guilty every time anything goes good for me."

It took one night to send Gina Connor's picture-perfect life into free-fall. And it will take one shattered soul to bring her back.

Gina never thought she'd be a widow in her 30s, but no one plans for drunk drivers. Six months is a long time to live a nightmare, and she's not sure she can make it another six.

Until Steven.

He's handsome, rude and everything she's been missing. One touch, and Gina was hooked. But guilt can't be pushed aside with a perfect kiss. Gina's husband is dead, but he's not gone.

And Steven is hiding something. A tortured past has left him scarred, and his secrets are catching up to them both. Danger was never Gina's favourite game, and she's not sure she wants to play.

Steven says he'll protect her, but who will protect him?

SAVIOUR OF THE SOUL

"I told her I was lost in this world and she smiled, because she was too. We were all lost somehow but we didn't care. We had, in each other's chaos, found each other." - Atticus.

Getting over the ultimate betrayal was easy because Steven was by her side, but now Gina faces the fight of her life.

A horrifying revelation will change everything Gina thought she knew about Steven. His past is much more devastating than she could ever comprehend.

A decades old vendetta threatens not only Gina's relationship with Steven, but also her life.

How much would you risk for the person you love? And what would they risk for you?

Saviour of the Soul will leave you in no doubt that blood isn't always thicker than water.

HEART AND SOUL

*"One word frees us from all the weight and pain of life.
That word is love."* - Sophocles

If the last few months have taught Gina anything, it's that life is full of surprises. Unfortunately, they're not all good ones.

After the death of her husband, a man she never dreamed would hurt her, she thought she'd never be truly happy again.

Then she met Steven Parker, a man with a complex and sometimes horrific past, and her life became complicated, dangerous even, as she was faced with events beyond her comprehension.

The saying "what doesn't kill you makes you stronger" certainly applies to their relationship and it appears the universe isn't finished with them yet. Dramatic changes in their personal lives and ghosts of relationships past threaten to derail Gina and Steven's path to happiness and will be the ultimate test of their love for each other.

BONUS

The following is an unedited, raw excerpt from my current WIP. Please note that anything from the title to the text may change by its eventual release date.

THE INTIMIDATION GAME
BOOK 1 IN THE GAME SERIES

Nikki Olsson left South Africa for Glasgow to escape a toxic relationship. To disappear into the background and start anew. But new opportunities bring their own problems and it seems her troubles have only just begun.

Landing in the world of corporate espionage was the last thing she had in mind but landing in Dan King's bed may be one step too far. He's a prominent figure in the corporate world and with vast wealth comes great power. He's also Nikki's boss and if the last year has taught her anything, it should be that this is not a road she wants to travel again.

CHAPTER 1

I WATCH HIM FROM my position in his bed. His shirt is pristine white, the collar starched to within an inch of its life. His suit is bespoke, obviously. God forbid he should wear anything off the peg. His hair products take pride of place on the dresser and as he pushes his hands through his salt and pepper strands, I realise how much I hate him. I am watching him with complete and utter contempt and am thankful that today is the day I get the hell away from this horrible controlling man.

"Nik you going to get up and make an effort today?"

Ugh I hate being called that and he knows it. *My name is Nikki*. His voice is making me feel nauseous. He's always so condescending towards me. I nod at him; I can't even begin to speak to him. I'm struggling to hold back my tears, but I will never cry in front of him again, it only serves to empower him.

I roll my eyes and sigh. He shakes his head and sneers at me, stalking towards where I lie. I move across the bed as quickly as I can but I'm not fast enough.

He grabs my jaw in one of his strong hands. His face is so close to mine and he talks quietly through gritted teeth. "Who the fuck do you think you are?"

I think my heart is about to burst out of my chest I'm so scared of him. I try to curl myself into a ball. If I make myself look smaller, he might relent.

He doesn't though, his grip simply gets stronger and my jaw is starting to hurt. "You're a lazy little bitch. You're nothing without me. Say it. Tell me I'm right."

I look at him wide eyed. I can't believe he's going to make me do this, but I know if I don't he won't leave, so I give him what he wants. "I'm a lazy little bitch." I can't form the words properly since my jaw feels like it is in a vice.

"And?" He shouts this time.

"And I'm nothing without you." My voice sounds so weak and pathetic.

His smile is nothing more than a nasty grin and I notice his pupils are huge. Oh my God, he's getting off on this.

"Fucking know your place you little idiot." He loosens his grip and pushes me back into the bed laughing to himself as he leaves the room.

I take a shuddering breath in and listen as he goes about his morning rituals. The coffee machine whirring, the clinking of the mugs and the fridge door opening and closing. When I hear the front door opening, I know he is giving himself a final check over in the mirror; narcissistic prick.

As soon as I hear the rumble of his precious Porsche, that he spends more time feeling up than me, I get out of bed and begin clearing him out of my life. Tears are blinding me, and I am sobbing so hard my chest hurts. I look at my reflection in the mirror. My face is red where he held it and my eyes look like sunken, sad pools. I am not giving him the satisfaction of an explanation; I just want to leave this whole part of my life behind. He has ruined me. My self-esteem is gone, and I constantly doubt myself. I should have left the first time he hit me.

I didn't actually want to realise there was anything wrong until I visited my sister Charlie in Scotland after she had her baby. My super observant sibling knew as soon as she set eyes on me that something wasn't right, but it was a very short conversation with her friend Gina that forced me admit to myself that this relationship is toxic.

As I picture Charlie giving me the evil eye when I told her I was fine, I smile. I'll be seeing her in a little over 24 hours and I'll never have to be back in South Africa again. It's the coward's way out, I know that, but I'm scared that if I tell him, that decision could ultimately end my life.

I don't even know how I ended up in this situation in the first place. I must have been so stupid and naive to even consider sleeping my way to a better job. My relationship with Michael started out as a casual fling. He was my immediate boss and was newly divorced at the time. He's also fifteen years older than me. I don't know why I listened to Mike when he said him getting a promotion would mean I would get to move up too, he said he'd make sure of that. I should have got out then but I had stupidly fallen for the creep and by the time he started to show his true colours I became too scared to leave him. Obviously I didn't move up in the company while he got promotion after promotion.

The fact that he was so much higher up the chain of command than me made my work life unbearable. He picked on me all the time and pulled me up on really trivial things. He always did it in front of people and told me that it was because he didn't want to arouse suspicion that we were in a relationship. As time went on, he started to act the same in private. My hair was never right, I wore too much make up, I didn't wear enough make up, I was too fat, I was too skinny, I was stupid, I dressed like a tramp, I dressed like a hooker. And the list goes on. I eventually got a new job elsewhere, but I just couldn't seem to leave him. My bruises are always well hidden, I've gotten good at that. And he has too. He knows where to hit me so that no one will ever see. So that no one will ever know what he really is.

When my parents decided they were moving back to the UK, I actually cried and begged them to take me with them. They thought I would stay since I had the perfect secure job and a 'nice' boyfriend. Little did they know? I think if my dad actually found out what Mike has done to me, he would kill him or have someone do it for him.

Knowing that I can get away from here without him finding out where I am is making me feel brave. I gather up all my belongings into my backpack, get dressed and have to stop myself making over the bed. That was another one of the things I could never get right. I leave, pulling the door shut behind me. As I push the silver key through the letterbox, I feel scared and liberated all at once.

"Good riddance you bastard," I whisper as I walk away from the house without looking back. I try my best to convince myself that the tears falling from my eyes now are happy ones.

CHAPTER 2

I NEVER THOUGHT OF Glasgow as being somewhere I would ever call home but having been here for five weeks and experiencing life on my own for the first time in my 26 years on this planet, I think I can safely say I do feel at home here. My sister Charlie was born here so I do have some distant connection.

My days have been filled with getting to know this very cosmopolitan city, my nights spent fretting about the new job I am starting today. My interview had been extremely short and sweet. I have a detailed work history and my former employer had put in a good word for me. It seemed as though the interview was purely a formality because I had an offer of employment in my inbox before I had even got back to Johannesburg.

Holding up two different dresses, the last of about forty, in front of me I try to decide which would fit with the feel of SecuriSoft. I am going to be heading up a newly formed team working on brand new security software. This is a major promotion for me and is the first time I'll be running a whole team of people. To say I'm nervous is an understatement; I'm petrified. I know how much first impressions matter and if I don't get it right it'll show and it's all I'll be known for.

My phone pings a text message and I'm startled since it's only four thirty in the morning. I see that the text is from my sister and my thoughts about who could be up at this time in the morning are sent packing.

Charlie says my niece is the spawn of the devil right now because she cries her little heart out at four every morning and as soon as she sees her mummy she smiles like, and I am quoting my sister here, she has just shit out a rainbow. Charlie has a real way with words but I love her dearly and I'm glad we are only forty miles apart now instead of almost six thousand. I put the dresses down on the bed and check the message.

Hey baby sis. Good luck today. I love you and I'm so proud of you. Devil baby loves you too.

C x

I laugh and hold the phone to my chest. My life has

changed in more ways than I ever imagined it would, but I feel that had it come any later I may not be standing in front of this mirror debating what dress to wear.

I still feel sick every time I think about my relationship with Mike: if you can even call it a relationship. The man is a controlling, nasty piece of work. I dread to think what his reaction was when he actually realised I had gone. When he realised he hadn't managed to break me completely.

But he did ruin me. I have no self-confidence, no belief in anything I can achieve. I look at myself in the mirror and I don't see the pretty blonde-haired young woman I am. I see a small insignificant shell of a person. Since I've been here, I've managed to put a mask on. These people don't know me; they don't know that I almost die inside any time a man speaks to me.

The shock of my phone ringing so loudly in my hand makes me jump and I throw it at the bed as if it has burned me. The screen flashes and the caller ID says the number is unknown. I can't bring myself to answer an unknown number yet. I put my hands over my ears and shut my eyes until it stops. It takes me a moment but I realise I'm screaming when I take my hands from my ears.

"Pull yourself together, bloody hell," I scold my

reflection. There's no message left.

This phone number I have is brand new, it's off the directory and I have my phone set to never share it when I call people except those in my contacts. It doesn't stop me worrying that someday, somehow he will find me. I don't know how long I'll look over my shoulder when I'm walking alone or how long I'll stop and let some innocent person pass me, when all they're doing is going about their business and happen to be walking behind me. I've lost count of the strange shops I've been in over the last while that I'd never go into just so that I could avoid someone being directly behind me.

I look at the dresses on the bed and give myself a mental slap. I need to get prepared to go into this office today and make the best first impression I possibly can.

***

My taxi driver has been chatting away since I got in the back of his cab and, while I've been listening and nodding along, I've taken nothing in. I feel like my brain is about to explode and I should be tired, but I happened to drink three cups of black coffee and a can of Red Bull for breakfast. I actually think I might have a heart attack at this rate.

As the taxi pulls up outside SecuriSoft's building, I steel myself with a steadying breath, pay the driver and get out of the cab. *It's now or never.*

I take in the building, which seems to look taller today than it did the last time I was here. The mirror glass front reflects the cloud spattered blue sky and the April sunshine is pleasant enough, albeit about fifteen degrees lower than I'm used to at this time of year.

I decided on a navy-blue shift dress and jacket ensemble and a pair of nude heels. My brand-new tan leather handbag that mum and dad gave me, as a good luck present, looks amazing with it. My long blonde hair is in a soft ponytail and I look professional. I look like I should be heading up my own team. I can do this.

The elevator that will take me to the third floor is empty. I press the number three button and as the doors close, I shut my eyes and take a deep breath.

The noise of the doors opening again startles me and I open my eyes as a scruffy looking, jeans and t-shirt clad guy gets in and presses number six.

He's standing too close to me so I move away a little trying to be as inconspicuous as I can. I can't stand my personal space being invaded like that. He smells goddamn divine. Damn it!

I stare at the ceiling and hold my bag in front of me like some sort of Viking shield. I can feel him looking at me, but I can't make eye contact with him. I'm starting to feel closed in and I think I'm going to have a panic attack. This is bloody ridiculous; I'd be better off living like a hermit.

Thank goodness the lift has reached the third floor and the doors open into a huge open plan space completely bathed in beautiful warm light with empty computer stations dotted all around. Scruffy guy stands aside and allows me to get off. I am forced to look at him and immediately wish I hadn't. He is like something off the cover of a rock album. He has tattoos on one arm and my God are those arms ripped. His scruffy stubble and messy dark brown hair give him a carefree look but those eyes. Wow. They are the deepest chocolate brown eyes I've ever seen. Scruffy Guy no more, now he's sexy Rock Star Guy.

"Th-thanks," I stutter and hurry out of the lift as quickly as my heels will allow. I don't even know where I'm supposed to be going. All I was told was third floor, nine am.

I look back at the lift as the doors close. Rock Star guy is gone. As I stand alone in the middle of the open area, I wonder what the hell I've let myself in for.

CHAPTER 3

"CAN I HELP YOU my love?" The voice from behind me makes me jump.

"Oh… ehm… sorry you startled me."

"Ooh you must be Nikki. I could tell by the South African accent. Nice to meet you I'm Damien Shaw but I prefer Damo." He holds out his hand.

"Eh, yeah I'm Nikki. It's nice to meet you Damien."

"Damo, please. I hate the name Damien it makes me feel like some sort of devil child. I think my bloody mother was in some sort of cult when she had me." He puts his hands on his hips and I regard him for a second.

He's slim built with flawless skin and coiffed brown hair. The most beautiful eyelashes I've ever seen on a man frame his huge blue eyes and I don't know why but I instantly like him. I feel comfortable with him. "Thanks for getting my accent by the way. Most of the time I'm mistaken for Australian or a New Zealander."

"I'm good with accents and don't worry I've been mistaken for being Irish before, even English. I mean come on, listen to me."

"So, Damo, I don't actually know who I'm supposed to be meeting here or actually what I'm doing. God I must sound ridiculous."

Damo waves his hand in the air. "No, you don't sound ridiculous. Astrid was supposed to call you on Friday and give you HR's contact name." Damo is interrupted by the click clack of heels. "Talk about shit and it hits you in the face," he whispers.

We both turn in the direction of the elevators and watch as a very tall, slim, blonde haired bombshell makes her way towards us. She walks like she's on a catwalk and must be about five foot ten in the heels she's wearing. She stops in front of us.

"Nikki?"

I nod. "Yes. Nice to meet you." I hold my hand out.

"Astrid Laurent," she says her surname with a French accent. "As in Yves Saint." She shakes my hand like she's the queen.

"Astrid you were supposed to call Nikki and let her know where she was to go this morning."

"Damo for fuck sake you know I had a big weekend. Anyway, I tried to phone her this morning. It's not my fault she didn't answer her phone." She talks as if I am invisible.

"Well there's a surprise. Come Nikki I'll take you down to HR and get you set up with your passes and stuff."

Astrid tuts and tosses her hair over her shoulder and saunters away from us. I'm a little shocked at her total lack of professionalism and I hope to God I don't have to manage her on my team.

Damo and I get into the lift and when the doors are shut, he sighs and shakes his head. "I'm sorry about her Nikki. She's a nasty piece of work. I honestly don't know why she's even still here. We all think she's sleeping with the boss. I suppose that's one way to keep your job or get promoted for doing nothing."

Oh my God his words make me want to run away. I feel tears surface in my eyes, and I can't stop them spilling over.

"God Nikki are you okay? I know she's a lot to take but you'll get used to ignoring her."

"I'm sorry Damo, I'm fine." I swipe the tears from my eyes and compose myself. "I'm just a little overwhelmed. I've never had a team of my own and I feel a little like a fish out of water here, but I'll get there honestly. Thanks for being so nice to me."

I'm taken aback when he hugs me. "We're going to be good pals you and me. I just know it Miss Nikki."

I smile as the doors open on the fifth floor and we make our way to HR. I'm glad I met Damo first and not Astrid.

***

My time at HR was short and sweet. They already had my badge and I.D card ready for me and they have given me an access fob for the office doors. I also have a pass card for the car park but since I don't have a car it's pretty useless right now. I need to start making money so that I can pay my own rent and not have to rely on the bank of mum and dad much longer. And it turns out Damien is actually my PA.

Back on the third floor I have been shown to what is my office although the open plan nature of this place means it really is just a space in the area with a desk and chair. Thankfully there is a small conference room that has walls and a door so at least it affords some privacy if needed.

Jed, my immediate line manager, has gathered the chatting, lively staff around my desk and I am about to be introduced to my team. I honestly hope I look composed because inside I'm dying.

"Right everyone," Jed raises his voice above the din and they all fall silent. Eight pairs of eyes give him their fullest attention. Astrid's are not one of them and I breathe an internal sigh of relief. Now I am left to wonder what her job actually is.

Damo winks at me as Jed begins my introduction. "So, guys this is Nikki Olsson, your team leader."

They all clap for me and I feel my cheeks heat.

"Nikki you can get to know everyone over this week, get a feel for the company and what we do and make yourself at home. This is your floor, if you need to make changes please feel free to do so."

I'm really not sure what I was expecting with this job. I knew it was heading up a new team working on new security software but I never imagined I'd have a whole floor of the building to myself. "Okay, um, thanks."

Jed asks everyone to give their name and their job title and they all smile at me as they each take it in turns to introduce themselves. The varying ages of the group is exciting to me. Many of the software companies I have known tend to favour very young people in their developer roles. I'm glad to see that this place challenges stereotypes. I think I'm going to be just fine here. I can't wait to get my teeth into this job now that I have met my team and this space I have to work in is excellent.

Jed leaves me to it and I watch him head for the elevator quickly followed by Astrid. She towers over him, her backside swinging from side to side as she goes. She is extremely beautiful, and she knows it.

"Hey Miss Nikki, how you feeling?" Damo plonks himself down on the chair on the other side of my desk.

"Oh, I'm fine, a little overwhelmed today but fine. Can I ask you, what does Astrid do here?"

"She's Jed's PA."

"She's not sleeping with him is she? He has a wedding ring on his finger."

Damo laughs. "No not Jed. God no he's so in love with his wife its vom inducing. No, I heard she's sleeping with Dan King, the big boss. Although it is only rumour and I think it actually stems from the fact that she's such a nasty bitch to everyone and, regardless of how many complaints are put forward about her, she's never been reprimanded."

"Oh. I haven't met Mr King yet. What's he like?"

He smiles. "He's a really great guy, don't know what the hell he sees in Astrid, and he doesn't like to be called Mr King. We don't really see him down here too often. His office is on the top floor, obviously. Wait till you see the view he has up there. Oh, and he's drop dead gorgeous. So, tell me Miss Nikki what's brought you to bonnie Scotland?"

I'm going to have to give him the edited version. I don't know him well enough to tell my shame to. "Well my mum and dad were moving back to the UK because of my dad's job and my sister lives in Edinburgh so I decided I didn't want to be the only one left in another continent."

"That's cool your sister lives here, you'll get to see her more often."

"Yeah and she's just had a baby, so I get to see my niece now too."

Damo claps his hands together. "Oh, I just love wee babies. They're so cute."

We are interrupted by the arrival of the elevator. It's Astrid and she's followed by Mr Rock Star. She makes her way to a desk at far end of the floor.

"I'm going to make a coffee Nikki would you like one?"

"No thanks Damo." I shake my head, but I can't take my eyes off Mr Rock Star. I watch as he walks to the desk Astrid is sitting at. He has his back to me, but I can see from his body language that he is angry with her. They are too far away for me to hear what they are saying. I'm starting to feel a little uncomfortable as I watch the look on Astrid's face change from indignation to what looks like fear. When he shoves her chair back with his foot and scatters her papers off the desk I want to die inside. I should help her, but I can't. I look around the room at the rest of my team and see that every one of them is engrossed in their computer screens and they all have ear pods or headphones on so none of them can actually hear what's going on.

I watch in stunned silence as Mr Rock Star stalks off to the elevator. The doors open immediately and he gets in. Still facing the back of the lift he lifts his fist and bangs it on the metal wall as the doors close on him.

That was a horrible thing to see. I don't think much of this guy now and I actually feel sorry for Astrid. She looks smaller now and not so full of herself anymore. I get up and go to her. I have to make sure she is okay.

"Astrid are you okay?" I ask as I near her desk.

She looks up at me and I see tears in her eyes. She quickly composes herself. "I'm fine. Why do you care?"

"Well no man has a right to talk to any woman like that and what he did was verging on assault. You really should tell someone about it. Get him disciplined. It's not right."

She eyes me suspiciously and then her demeanour changes. Her eyes soften and she looks sincere. "Oh Nikki I can't. He's further up the chain than me and I worry I might lose my job if I complain. Could you speak to Mr King for me? I'd be so grateful."

"Of course I will. What's his name?"

"Darren Keane."

"I'm going to get this sorted for you right now. Will

you be okay?"

She nods and smiles at me, her tears all but gone. "Thanks Nikki, you're too kind."

I head for the elevator feeling rather pleased with myself that I am helping someone who is obviously going through the same mental torture I did at the hands of a man. I hit the twelfth floor button and wonder to myself what Mr King is like.

The Intimidation Game is provisionally scheduled to be released in Autumn 2019.

THANK YOU

I hope you've enjoyed reading the Soul Series. It was such a great project to work on and I am so grateful to everyone for their support.

DON'T FORGET

A review or rating from readers is always appreciated. In fact, they can be crucial for Indie Authors like me so I'd be more than grateful if you could leave a rating on which ever outlet you bought my books from. As always, I appreciate and read every single one of them.

Claire x

Printed in Great Britain
by Amazon